COUNTRY LIFE

Ruth Deacon has always wanted to set up a wildlife sanctuary and rescue centre, and now her dream has finally come true. Her neighbours at the McMillan farm don't seem keen, though when she meets Tom McMillan, she thinks she might win them over.

But someone is aiming to destroy the reputation of the centre. And the farm manager accuses her of dumping rubbish which has injured one of their calves. Ruth is sure that Tom will believe she has nothing to do with it. However, when he shows doubt, she wonders if they really know each other at all . . .

SARAH PURDUE

COUNTRY
LIFE

Complete and Unabridged

LINFORD
Leicester

First published in Great Britain in 2020

First Linford Edition
published 2023

*A catalogue record for this book is available
from the British Library.*

ISBN 978–1–4448–5104–5

Published by
Ulverscroft Limited
Anstey, Leicestershire

Printed and bound in Great Britain by
TJ Books Ltd., Padstow, Cornwall

This book is printed on acid-free paper

Unexpected Visitor

Ruth hammered the post one last time and stood back to admire her handiwork. The sign *Deacon's Wildlife Sanctuary and Hospital* was set into the grass verge alongside the country lane.

'Well, what do you think?' she asked, turning to look at Joe who stood beside her.

'A little wonky, but I like it,' Joe said, a grin nearly hidden behind his heavy grey beard.

'I can't believe we've actually done it,' Ruth said, smiling at the sign.

'You did, Ruthie. This is all you. All your hard work.'

'I had a lot of help,' Ruth said, looking at Joe and hoping he understood how grateful she was for all his support in getting the smallholding and wildlife sanctuary running and ready for its first patients. Joe shrugged.

'It's not like I don't have the time, Ruthie.'

Ruth reached out and squeezed his arm. She knew that no words could provide him comfort but she wanted to let him know that she was there for him.

'The main centre will start transferring animals tomorrow. I'll come over with the first lot so we can get them settled in.'

Ruth stepped back on to the grass verge as the sound of a truck making its way along the road met her ears.

'Look out — it's the neighbours,' Joe said with a snort.

The vehicle was unmistakable. It was a working farm truck but despite that it was as clean as it would have been the day it rolled out of the factory. The logo on the side was unmistakable: *McMillan Family Farm*. The truck slowed down and Ruth held up a hand to give a friendly wave but all she got in return was a heavy scowl from the driver, an older man who made Ruth feel like she had insulted him deeply but had no idea why.

'No thawing of relations, then,' Joe said but he didn't sound that bothered.

Ruth watched the truck drive off and turn in to a lane about a quarter of mile down the road. She sighed.

'I'm really not sure why they're so upset, it's barely twenty acres of land. Their farmland covers half the county.'

'Only because they've been buying all the land they can for years.' Joe snorted with derision. 'And they have the cheek to call it a family business.' Joe signed quotes in the air. 'Old McMillan would turn in his grave if he could see what that boy of his was doing.'

Ruth nodded. Joe had lived in the area since he was a child and had at one time worked for the McMillans, or at least the previous generation.

'Well, hopefully they'll get over it.'

Joe flashed her a look that told her she would be waiting a long time for that to happen.

'They can't object to the wildlife hospital, can they?'

'They'll object to anything that stands in the way of them making a profit. But you can't let that worry you, Ruthie. Not

3

only are you doing a great thing but it's what you've always wanted.'

Ruth nodded. She had hoped to get on with the neighbours and, because they had bought up most of the land around, they were pretty much the only neighbours.

'Yep, enough about them — we have loads to do if we're going to be ready for our first patients.'

Ruth had been up since five. She was used to being an early riser with her previous job and it was a hard habit to break. And soon she would have lots of animals to care for, so long lie-ins would become a thing of the past.

The smallholding had a small, ramshackle cottage. It hadn't been extended since it was built so still had the original two rooms, but to Ruth it was perfect. She had a wood-burning stove which created a warm and cosy kitchen/living space and then a small bedroom, which although it had no heating still managed to feel cosy. The past owner, George, had installed a tiny bathroom in one corner of the bedroom which contained a shower and a toilet in its very tight space.

Ruth cradled her cup of tea and opened the front door, before stepping out into the spring morning. It was still dark, of course, but she could just about make out the new shelters that she and Joe had put together.

The smallholding had a sort of yard, with a dry stone wall encircling it and an old barn that had seen better days. Joe had been able to patch up the holes in the roof so that it would be watertight for any new residents. What she couldn't see were the field and meadows that lay beyond the yard that were also hers.

There was a small vegetable garden beyond the dry stone wall that had seen better days. George had been unable to keep up with it in the last few years. She smiled, thinking of George.

She was fairly sure that the McMillans had offered way more money than she had been able to, but she knew that George was determined that his land would remain as a smallholding and not get absorbed by the biggest land owner in the county.

If she could find the time, she wanted to restore his vegetable garden. She had promised George that he could come back and visit whenever he wanted and she hoped that he would.

Ruth felt movement beside her and she leaned down to ruffle the hair of Poppy, her Labrador-sized dog of unknown parentage.

'Well, I'm impressed that you managed to pull yourself away from your new favourite spot,' Ruth said softly.

It seemed that Poppy was in love with the place, particularly now her bed was right next to the stove. Poppy leaned into Ruth's leg.

'I think we're going to be happy here, Pops.'

Poppy made a quiet rumbling sound in her chest which Ruth took to be agreement.

'We should get breakfast. It's going to get busy around here soon.'

Ruth stood up to move inside but

Poppy was frozen to the spot. Ruth peered into the darkness but could make out nothing.

'What is it, girl?' she asked softly, feeling the hackles on the back of the dog's neck rise like furry armour. Poppy didn't move but continued to stare at something Ruth couldn't see.

'Hello?' Ruth called, suspecting that if it was a visiting badger or fox it would run away at the sound of her voice. She strained her ears but could hear nothing.

Poppy grumbled again in her throat. Whatever it was, it wasn't running away. Ruth could feel a small prickle of fear which she pushed away. She wasn't afraid of whatever could be out there, it was probably just an animal.

'Hello?' she said again, louder this time and then a large shape loomed out of the gloom.

Not a Great Start

'Hello,' Ruth said softly once she was sure her heart wouldn't leap out of her chest. She forced herself to take a slow, deep breath and held her hand out to the figure in front of her. She had seen its long horns first and that it given her a start but as it had moved towards her it materialised into a soft face and large shaggy body. It was a cow, though not a full-grown one, judging from its coat. It mooed in a melancholy way.

'You're OK, buddy,' Ruth said, moving slowly towards it until she could reach out and stroke its side. Poppy whined.

'It's all right, Pops, she's just a baby and a lost one at that.'

Ruth moved her hand and felt for the tag in the young cow's ear. Not that she needed to do, there was only one place that the cow could have come from and that was McMillan's.

'How did you get lost?' she said softly to the cow. 'Everyone will be worried about you.'

Ruth moved over to one of the small sheds and flipped on the outside light, before opening the shed door. Inside was a fresh layer of straw, ready for any larger patients that might come her way but right now it seemed the perfect place to keep the cow until it could be collected. All she had to do was persuade the cow.

Fifteen minutes later and Ruth had worked up a sweat. She liked to think that she could build up a rapport with any animal but now she was having serious doubts as to her ability as a 'cow whisperer'.

The cow didn't seem unhappy, she just wasn't prepared to move from her spot. She had found a nice patch of fresh grass and was happily munching away.

Standing in her pyjamas, with a jacket pulled over the top to keep out the worst of the early morning chill, Ruth sighed. She had tried to look up a phone number for McMillan's but her phone signal was sketchy at best and was not up to doing the internet thing this morning.

9

What she didn't need on her first day open, was a rather large cow wandering around, getting up to mischief. Poppy had obviously decided that the cow was no longer a threat and was curled up by the front door, watching Ruth's efforts. It was clear to Ruth that Poppy would never be a working farm dog.

The problem was, Ruth wanted to go and get showered and dressed but with the cow roaming free, she was too worried that she would get up to mischief that would not play out well with the neighbours.

'Come on, please? The shed is nice and cosy and then I can see about getting you back home.'

The cow blinked its huge eyelashes at her but it was clear that she had no intention of moving from her spot. Ruth turned to look at Poppy, as if she might have a better idea.

Poppy was back on her feet and looking out beyond the courtyard area with her nose in the air. Ruth turned to look and a small, wiry black-and-white

10

sheepdog appeared. It took one look at the cow and then barked, before sitting down and looking expectantly at Ruth.

'Hello,' Ruth said to the dog. 'Are you lost, too, or have you come looking for your cow?'

The dog tilted its head to one side and then barked again. Ruth wondered if that was the dog's way of telling the cow off.

There was a high-pitched whistle and the sheepdog's ears pricked up. There was another series of whistles and the dog waited until they had finished and then barked again as a figure appeared in the gloom.

'Matilda, how did you get here?'

The sheepdog trotted up and sat beside the man. Ruth could now make out that it was Thomas McMillan, the heir to the McMillan farms.

He looked as if he had been awake all night, but he was smartly dressed in cords, a checked shirt and the obligatory waxed jacket.

'Hello — sorry, did we wake you?' Tom said and Ruth could tell that he had seen her rabbit pyjamas.

'No, we were up,' Ruth said, hoping the half-light would hide her blush. She had no reason to be embarrassed since it was still basically dark and most people would still be in bed but still she felt it all the same.

'Poppy and I came out for a leg stretch before getting ready for the day and then we met Matilda here.'

'I am so sorry,' he said. 'She managed to squeeze through the tiniest gap in the fence.' He ran an expert hand over the cow's back as if he were checking her for injuries. 'She does seem to have a bit of the spirit of adventure about her. I'm Tom, from McMillan's.'

'Ruth,' Ruth said, although she knew that they both knew who each other were. This was the first time they had actually met in person. 'Not a problem. I did try to find your phone number so I could give you a call but I don't have enough signal.'

Tom nodded.

'It's not great up here, although I kind

of like it that way, you know. I enjoy not being contactable every second of the day.'

Tom was too lost in checking Matilda over to see the surprise on Ruth's face. Somehow she hadn't expected him to want to be cut off. From what she had seen of his farm, it had been all modern equipment and to her mind no soul but here he was saying what she would have said if asked that question.

Being disconnected was one of the things that she loved about being in the country, unless you needed to look up a farmer's phone number, of course.

'Why don't you let me have your number? Then I can text you mine so if we have any more itinerant cattle you can call me.' Tom was smiling and so Ruth pulled out her phone and typed in the number as he said it out loud. She sent him a quick text and he replied.

'I was trying to get her into one of my sheds, so I could keep her from wandering further away,' Ruth said, indicating the shed's open door.

'She's a stubborn one, as well as an adventurer,' Tom said with a smile of affection.

'I didn't realise you had cattle,' Ruth said, feeling suddenly curious about this man that she had heard so much about, most of which didn't seem to match the person standing in front of her.

'This is more of a hobby. The farm is mainly arable but I missed the animals so I reintroduced a few rare breeds.'

Ruth nodded, again feeling surprised.

'She's a beauty,' Ruth said as the cow nudged against her.

'Our first baby, so she's pretty special. I hope she didn't cause any damage,' Tom said. Ruth could see that thought had only just occurred to him as he looked up and scanned the yard.

'No, it's fine, she was just eating some grass that could do with cutting back.'

Tom nodded and for the first time they locked eyes and it was as if neither of them wanted to look away. The sheep-dog let out a small bark.

'Colin's right, of course. We shouldn't

14

take up more of your time.'

'Colin?' Ruth asked with a smile that was returned.

'My goddaughter Tessa named him. She thought it was funny.'

'An excellent name,' Ruth said in mock seriousness to Colin, whose tongue was lolling out in what she took to be approval.

'Are you opening today?' Tom asked.

Ruth smiled.

'We're getting some of the longer-term rehab patients over today from the main hospital and then it will just be a case of waiting to see what people bring in.'

'Well, good luck,' Tom said and he appeared to mean it. He had a halter in his hand, which he slipped over Matilda's neck and he clicked his tongue. Matilda reluctantly turned away from the grass and started to move.

'Thanks,' Ruth said somewhat belatedly. Tom turned and flashed her a smile as he, Matilda and Colin walked off in the direction of his farm.

'And I love the pyjamas!' His voice

carried across the darkness.

All Ruth could do was stand and stare, not that she could see them, although she could hear Matilda mooing the odd complaint. Tom was not at all what she had expected.

The McMillan farm had been painted as the bad guy, by both George and Joe. She trusted them both completely but perhaps they saw the farm as one big entity rather than getting to know the individuals themselves?

Tom seemed friendly and certainly had shown no signs of being against the wildlife sanctuary. Not to mention the fact that he was also handsome in a sort of posh farmer kind of way.

'Well, that went better than I expected,' Ruth said to Poppy as she turned to walk towards the cottage. Poppy looked up at her and Ruth could swear that she was smiling.

'I take it from that dopey look on you face that you liked him, too. Or was it Colin that caught your eye?'

Poppy grumbled and Ruth thought

16

that if it was possible, her dog was actually embarrassed.

'Well enough of that, young lady, we have to get up and get ready. It's going to get busy around here very shortly.'

Ruth was not wrong. By lunchtime she had in residence three badgers at various stages of recovery, a fox and a whole host of hedgehogs who needed time to put weight on before they could be released back into the wild.

The small aviary had a blackbird and a robin in, which would be released in a few weeks as they were both recovering well from wing damage. She had booked each animal in, given them a quick health check and settled them in their new temporary accommodation.

'Well, that's it for now,' Joe said as he walked out of the open front door of the cottage, carrying two mugs of tea.

'Well, hopefully word has got round to the local villages that we are here and able to take animals directly,' Ruth said. She wanted to be involved in the rehab of animals treated at the main site but

17

also wanted to reduce the stressful journey time for animals who were local.

'Ruthie, we put posters up everywhere. Everyone knows you're here and I'm sure as soon as they have something for you, they'll be here. After all, spring tends to be our busiest time.'

'Thanks for all your help today,' Ruth said before taking a sip of tea.

'We're a team, Ruthie, and I'll be here helping you out as often as you'll have me.'

'Help in exchange for a cooked meal seems like it's more in my favour than yours,' Ruth said with a smile, although in truth she would feed him whether he helped out or not. He hadn't been doing so well since losing his wife but setting up the new site seemed to have given him a fresh purpose.

'Wouldn't want to be anywhere else,' Joe said and Ruth could see all that he couldn't say in his eyes. She reached over and squeezed his arm.

'Quick tea break and then I'm going to get on with getting the pasture ready,' he added. 'You never know when we might need it for deer — although I'm hoping that we might get to rehome the donkey and her pony friend.'

'Me, too,' Ruth said. The donkey and her best friend were at the main site. Both had been rescued in a terrible state. They'd had no offers to adopt them both as yet and didn't want to separate them so Ruth had suggested that they spend their retirement at hers.

'I'll make us some lunch whilst you get started and I'll help you after.'

Putting up the fence was hard work. Between them they had managed to sink a small row of fence posts but it was going to be some time before they would be ready for larger guests. Although the day was cool, Ruth had once again worked up pink cheeks and had removed her jacket. The sounds of a vehicle pulling into the yard made her turn.

'Maybe we have our first official patient,' Ruth said to Joe but his face was fixed and he looked away.

'I doubt it, Ruthie. Looks like the

neighbours have found something to complain about.'

As the car parked up, Ruth could make out the signage which indicated the car was one of a fleet of vehicles that belong to the McMillan farm.

'I didn't tell you that I met Tom this morning. He seemed really nice,' Ruth said, not making eye contact with Joe for fear she might give away just how nice she had thought he was.

'Tom's not the one you should be worried about.'

A figure climbed out of the car and Ruth could see instantly that it wasn't Tom. It was a man, but he was older and had greying hair. Ruth had seen him in the truck with Tom the day before when they had driven past and the older man was wearing the same expression, as if something had offended him deeply.

'You there!' he shouted as if Ruth was on his land without permission.

'Can I help you?' Ruth asked, keeping her voice polite. She wanted to get on with her neighbours and if this man worked for Tom then she would give him some leeway with his manners.

'I've come to tell you that we won't tolerate theft,' the man said as Ruth blinked in surprise.

'Excuse me?' she said and this time didn't manage to keep her voice quite so even.

'You heard me. I'm no fool.'

'What exactly is it that you think you have lost?' Ruth injected some steely calm to her voice. An accusation was not something she was prepared to take.

'Our prize cattle are worth a fortune and I've no doubt that someone such as you has looked up how much you could sell one for.'

'Wait, are you talking about Matilda?'

'Do you see other prize cattle around here?' the man sneered. He had walked closer now but Ruth stood her ground, Joe standing a few steps behind her.

'I found Matilda this morning, on my land,' Ruth said the words slowly, 'and Tom came and took her home. He said that she had squeezed through a gap in the fence.'

The older man looked disparagingly at her.

'Tom might be prepared to overlook the obvious but I'm not. There's no way that cow could have 'escaped' without help.' His emphasis on the word 'escaped' was not lost on Ruth.

She looked him in the eye. She had had enough.

'Well, if that's the case she had no help from me. You may not have noticed the sign but we are a wildlife hospital and rehabilitation centre. Domestic cattle are not really our thing.'

The man looked around the yard in disgust, as if saving wildlife was freakish thing to do.

'If you want to 'save' vermin that's your business but if any of your work has an impact on the farm, we will take action.'

Ruth raised an eyebrow. There was no way she was going to give into a bully like this. She had met people like him before, people who put money before everything, people, animals, the environment. He was entitled to his opinions but then so was she.

'Since your cattle was on my land, I would say it was more likely that the problem was the other way round, wouldn't you?'

'Not if she had help,' he snapped back.

'Then I suggest you go and find out who helped her and stop wasting my time.'

'I'll be watching,' he said with one last glare before he stalked off to his truck and drove away, too fast for Ruth's liking.

She let out her held in breath. This was not the relationship she wanted with her neighbour but if he had made up his mind about her, she doubted she would be able to change it.

'He's a nasty piece of work,' Joe said, with a growl.

'Who is he exactly?' Ruth asked, turning back to face him.

'Farm foreman — he worked for old McMillan. I think he's some kind of distant relation but always gives the impression he's the boss.'

'I'm surprised Tom keeps him on, with an attitude like that.'

'The Lord of the Manor knows all about him,' Joe said dismissively. Ruth frowned. She still couldn't see how her impression of Tom was so different. 'Always sends him to do his dirty work.'

'But this morning Tom said it was their fault that Matilda had managed to squeeze through a gap in the fence.'

'He probably did until Jeremy started whispering his poison. It was Jeremy who objected so strongly to you buying the land. Tried to get the neighbouring villages onside to keep you out but they won't be doing anything he tells them to. Too much history there.'

Ruth knew in that instant that Jeremy and Joe had butted heads before. For all she knew, Jeremy could be the reason he left the farm, after working there for many years. One thing was for certain, Joe wasn't going to be any help in creating positive relations with their neighbours.

Something that Ruth thought was still possible, if her first impressions of Tom had been anything to go by. All she needed to do was come up with some kind of plan.

'Well, since we will be wanting to release some wildlife locally, it would be helpful if we can get them onside,' Ruth said.

'You've as much chance of winning over Jeremy as I have of winning the lottery and you know I don't go in for gambling,' Joe said darkly as he picked up his mallet and started to hammer in another fencing post.

'Well, maybe Jeremy isn't the answer. Tom seemed mildly interested in what we are doing.'

Joe's answer to that was a snort but Ruth wasn't going to let that put her off. If you lived in the countryside then you needed to be at least on speaking terms with your neighbours, since you never knew when you might need some help.

'We just need to get them to see how important wildlife is to their farm as well as everything else.'

'He ain't interested, Ruthie. It's all about the money for them.'

'I don't think that's true of Tom. You should have seen him with Matilda . . .'

'Ruthie, I don't think we are going to agree on this so maybe we should just focus on getting the paddock ready.'

Ruth nodded. She certainly didn't want to fall out with Joe. He was her only full-time volunteer and she valued his friendship. No, she would just have to try to sort this one out on her own.

Terrible Accusations

Two days later and Ruth had still had no chance even to think up a plan. She had been worried that they were too far out in the countryside for most people to find them, let alone bring them wildlife, but her concerns were unfounded. The two nearest villages some seven and 10 miles away had embraced the concept with gusto and, as was the norm for this time of year, the hospital was nearly full to capacity with spring babies.

They had so many baby birds that Ruth had lost count and was now having to feed them every hour all through the night. Not that she was complaining — this was why she had worked so hard to set the sanctuary up in the first place.

Today, some volunteers from the main centre had come over to help and seemed keen to take on some of the night shifts. They also had a few more hedgehogs to add to the collection, a litter of fox cubs and one very tiny weasel that Joe had named Pop.

The other good thing had been that some of the villagers had expressed an interest in helping out, and Ruth had arranged to do an induction day at the weekend to get them up to speed.

'You look like you could do with a cuppa,' Joe said, a grin on his face, along with a few streaks of dirt.

'I'd love one, but I can make it. You're the one who has been building fences all day.'

'It's done, Ruthie, and you know I'm like a pig in muck. I told you this place would take off.'

'You weren't wrong,' Ruth said with a smile. 'Are you still OK to help out on Saturday? The induction is going to take up quite a bit of time.'

'Of course, love. I'll even do some baking so we can have some cake for the volunteers.'

'Only if you have time. I can do some.' By that, Ruth meant drive to the village and clear out the bakery.

'I think we both know that's probably best left to me. Whilst I love your dinners, you're not a natural baker.'

Ruth laughed. Having Joe around made her not miss her dad so much and she knew that Joe needed the company, too.

'I've put a stew in the slow cooker this morning. Your favourite chicken and veg.'

'Dumplings?' Joe asked.

'Of course.'

'I'll go make the tea, love. Why don't you sit yourself down for a minute?'

Ruth eased her aching body on to the wooden bench that she had set up outside the cottage, with the best view of the courtyard. She had been so run off her feet, she had barely been able to take in the fact that her dream was becoming a reality around her.

She had done it — with a lot of help — but she had done it and she knew her dad would be proud. Her mind wandered and she started to think about Tom, appearing in the gloom, looking for his first calf.

She was sure that Joe was wrong about him. She was sure it was possible to have a working relationship between the sanctuary and the farm and maybe more, her mind pointed out. Just the thought of it made her blush and she pushed down the feelings.

That was not important and it wasn't as if she would have the time. No, she needed to concentrate on the sanctuary and getting the neighbours onside. She pulled out her mobile and sent a quick text.

'Hi, Tom. It's Ruth from the wildlife sanctuary. We're having a volunteer open day on Saturday and I thought you might like to pop by and see some of the work we are doing. No need to let me know, just come by if you fancy it.'

She pressed send before she could change her mind.

Ruth had to work hard not to check her phone continually to see if he had replied. She didn't really understand why she was doing it, since she was not that kind of person. Deep down she knew that she had felt something when she met Tom and she had an inkling that he might have felt something, too.

None of that was an excuse for her to lose her head or lose sight of what she was trying to achieve at the sanctuary. She had worked too hard and too long not to give it her all.

Ruth left the phone on the bench. It was turned up to full volume, as it was the number for the sanctuary as well as her personal phone and she didn't want to miss any calls about animals in need of help.

When Joe came out with the tea, Ruth was doing her rounds, checking in on how the bird feeding was going. The two experienced volunteers from the centre, Barbara and Sam, seemed to have a routine.

'It's a bit like painting the Forth Bridge,' Ruth said through the fine mesh that covered the window to the bird shed.

Barbara looked up with a smile.

'Ah, but Sam and I have it down pat.

31

And we're loving every minute of it.' She smiled warmly at Ruth.

'I can't thank you enough for your help. The birds alone are a full time job.'

'One that doesn't let you sleep, either,' Sam said as she noticed the dark circles under Ruth's eyes. 'But we've sorted a rota, at least for the next few nights. You should be able to get some sleep.'

'You are both wonderful,' Ruth said and felt a little teary.

Both Barbara and Sam had promised to help out as much as they could when she had first floated the idea of buying the smallholding and setting up the sanctuary but she had never imagined that they would come through as well as they had.

'Your dad would be mighty proud of you,' Barbara said softly.

Ruth could only nod in reply. This had always been her dad's dream. She had shared that dream ever since she was a little girl, helping him to care for the wildlife they had room for in their tiny back garden.

He hadn't lived to see it, but she had told him all about her plans and he had seemed confident that she would be able to pull it off.

And she wouldn't have been able to do it without him. He had left her the small house and the benefits from his job as a postie. It wasn't a fortune but it was enough to get up and running, and she reckoned that if she was careful with the money left, it would give her three years without needing to find additional employment to cover the bills.

'I hope so,' she said softly, trying to swallow the lump in her throat.

'He would,' Joe said, appearing beside her with a tray of tea. 'He talked about your and his dream often enough and this is it, love, take my word for it.'

Ruth helped herself to a cup and used it as an excuse to hide her face for a moment as she tried to rein in all she was feeling. She was tired, she knew, and that wasn't helping in the grand scheme of things.

Joe opened the door to the bird shed

and closed it behind him, before opening the second door which prevented any fledglings escaping before they were truly ready, and handed around the tea.

From his pocket he produced a packet of biscuits and was rewarded with a kiss on the cheek from Barbara.

'Martin and Jen are taking over in an hour. Why don't you go and sit down, Ruth? Then we can have a quick meeting to discuss catering for Saturday and you can have the evening off.'

Ruth nodded and smiled. There was no point arguing with Sam. She had learned that lesson years ago when she first started helping out at the main centre. Sam had raised five boys and what she said was law.

Ruth scooped up the phone and walked back to the cottage, cradling her cup of tea. She couldn't resist a quick peek in at the hedgehogs, who were all curled up in balls, asleep.

She was sure that they could get enough weight on all of them to release them in the summer, as long as they continued in the way they were going.

The cottage door was open and Poppy appeared to greet her. Together they walked over to the two-seater sofa between the wall and the stove and curled up together. Ruth's phone beeped.

'I don't know whether I want it to be him or not,' she whispered to Poppy. Poppy whined in response and Ruth's suspicion that her dog had developed a soft spot for the lovely sheepdog, Colin, was confirmed.

'I can tell him to bring Colin, if you like,' Ruth said with a grin. Poppy laid her head on Ruth's lap and gave the impression of being a lovesick teenager, all big eyes and dopey smile.

Ruth opened her phone and stared.

She read and reread the message, still not being able to compute what it was saying.

A shadow appeared in the doorway.

'I was hoping to get to you before you saw it,' Joe said and behind him Ruth could see a worried looking Barbara.

'Who would have done this?' Ruth

said. The tears she had tried to fight back earlier were back again but this time with a feeling of intense anger.

'Everyone who knows you will know it's not true,' Barbara said, stepping into the small room and moving Poppy so she could sit next to Ruth on the small sofa.

'There's no name to it. Typical coward and bully. Posting some nonsense and not being man enough to say who they are.'

'What do I do?' Ruth said, looking from Barbara to Joe. 'I'd never steal money from the charity, you both know that.' She looked at them closely, needing to know that they believed her.

'Of course you didn't!' Sam said brusquely, appearing in the doorway. 'I'm the treasurer and have just posted to say as much.' Her eyes flashed with anger but when she saw the look on Ruth's face, they softened a little.

'I do the books for the main charity and your new charity, love. I can categorically say it's not true.'

'Some people might believe it, though,'

Barbara said. 'Surely they've committed some kind of libel?'

'They have but there'll be no way of proving who is was although I think we can all take a good guess at the most likely suspect,' Joe said, his voice filled with anger.

'Can't we report it to the police?' Barbara asked, ignoring the inference. Everybody by now knew how Joe felt about Jeremy.

'Not sure it will do much good, but probably best to make them aware,' Sam said. 'And I'm going to get on to Derek. He runs the local website — he shouldn't be allowing people to post messages like that.'

Joe snorted.

'He'll love the extra attention. He's a wannabe if ever I met one.'

'Maybe we should just ignore it,' Ruth said, suddenly wishing it would all just go away. 'Perhaps if we say nothing, if we rise above it, people will realise that there is no truth to it.'

'People like gossip, love. It's a sad fact

but you don't need to say anything. I will post the message since I am in the best position to refute it,' Sam said.

'But what if they try and drag you into it?' Ruth asked, suddenly worried for her friend.

'Let them try,' Sam said, her eyes flashing. 'Just let them try.'

Saturday morning brought with it a perfect spring day, sunny and with blue skies but not so warm that they would need to think about providing shade.

Ruth finished tying the balloons to the sign and sent up one more prayer that people would actually turn up to the volunteers' open day.

Sam had posted a message on the local website and in no uncertain terms called the anonymous person out, but would it be enough?

Ruth felt a surge of frustration at the unfairness of it all. It was so easy these days to ruin a person's reputation and to do it at a distance with no right of reply. You could say what you want and damage lives in the process.

Her friends had rallied round, of course, but the number of phone calls and people bringing in injured and young animals had seemed to drop. Joe told her it was usual after the initial rush but Ruth couldn't help wondering if the anonymous accuser had anything to do with it.

Did the local people now not trust her? It was a painful thought.

'Right, love, where do you want these?' Sam asked, waving the bright yellow plastic donation boxes.

Ruth winced.

'I'm still not sure that's a good idea. What if people do come and think I'm just in it for the money?'

Sam rolled her eyes.

'Nobody runs a wildlife charity to get rich and anyone with half a brain knows that you end up living as frugally as possible so you can use any spare money that is actually yours to keep the business afloat.'

Sam put down the donation boxes and placed a hand on each shoulder so that

Ruth had to look her in the eye.

'Ruth, you have done nothing wrong and you are not going to let some lowlife bully affect how you care for the animals, are you?'

Ruth shook her head. When Sam said it out loud all it all made perfect sense but the dull ache of worry just wouldn't go away.

'We are asking for small donations for the coffees and cakes. And I will personally reassure everyone that the money will go directly into the charity funds, where any withdrawals are co-signed by the trustees.'

'What if he posts another message?' Ruth asked. She didn't know why she was calling the poster a 'he'. Joe may have convicted Jeffrey in his absence but Ruth wasn't quite prepared to do that just yet, even if he did seem like the most likely candidate. She just couldn't believe that Tom could have someone like that working for him.

'Then I will reply and if necessary we will get an independent accountant to review the books and publish his report,' Sam said with a flourish and Ruth knew that she was right. They had done nothing wrong and Ruth needed to start acting like it.

'OK, thanks, Sam, for the pep talk — and everything else.'

Sam grinned.

'My pleasure, love,' she said before striding away to find the best spots for the donation boxes. Ruth watched her go. It was always good to be reminded how lucky you could be when you found a new family.

At two o'clock the place was full, or at least it felt that way. There were lots of faces that were familiar to Ruth and she knew they lived locally. Even Abby, the landlady of the local pub, had put in a brief appearance before returning to open up for the afternoon.

'Told you it would be all right,' Sam said, walking up to stand by Ruth with a triumphant grin.

'I should listen to you more and worry less,' Ruth said returning the smile.

'And I haven't had one person ask me about where the money goes so they have all proved themselves to be sensible people who don't listen to malicious gossip.'

Ruth nodded and scanned the crowds. Everyone seemed to be enjoying themselves. Ruth had spoken to at least ten people who would like to give up some of their time and been able to conduct everyone on a guided tour of both the facilities and the current residents.

'Barbara and I will be starting the bird induction in ten minutes, if that's all right with you? I've had a few people say they would be interested in joining the rota.'

'Perfect, thank you,' Ruth said. 'I'll take over the teas and cake stand.'

Sam nodded her approval and then went to collect Barbara, before announcing loudly to the crowd that the bird induction would start shortly.

Ruth took her place behind the small trestle table that they had set up near to the cottage, so that the extension cord for the water urn could run back to a suitable plug. She watched as Joe explained to a group of young children that the paddock might have its first resident soon, in the form of a donkey.

Of course there was one face that she had looked for but had yet to see. Tom had not replied to her text and there was no sign that he was going to take up her offer of visiting the site.

Ruth felt slightly embarrassed, wondering if she had detected friendliness in Tom that simply wasn't there. He had seemed interested in what she was trying to do but maybe he was just feigning politeness?

Maybe he shared Jeremy's opinion? She shook her head. That she could not believe. It was clear that Jeremy hated the idea of the sanctuary but that did not ring true with the image of Tom she had in her mind.

'No-one who liked rabbit pyjamas could possibly hate wildlife,' she muttered to herself. A shadow fell over her and she looked up.

Tom was standing in front of her but all she could think was whether he had heard what she had just said.

A Dinner Invitation

His face gave it away. She just knew that he had heard every word and was no doubt making the connection to their previous meeting. Thankfully the sun was out and so Ruth could only hope that he would interpret her blush as being busy working in the sun.

'Tom, good to see you,' Ruth said in a voice that sounded way too hearty. She masked her further state of embarrassment with a smile, which was returned.

'Looks like you've a great turn out,' Tom said looking around, which Ruth thought was probably an opportunity for her to get her act together.

'It was supposed to be a volunteer induction day but it's turned into more of an open day. I have to admit I didn't think that many people would be interested. It's wonderful,' she added, thinking she might have sounded like she was complaining when in fact she was feeling the exact opposite.

'Oh, I don't know — I think most people who live in the countryside have an affinity for its wildlife.'

Ruth had an image of Jeremy in her mind and wondered if Tom knew how strongly his farm manager felt about the sanctuary. When Tom turned back to face her she thought he probably didn't — either that it he was exceptionally good at hiding his thoughts.

'They certainly seem to,' Ruth said, deciding that she had spent enough time reliving the confrontation with Jeremy.

'Have lots of people signed up to help?' Tom asked.

'Yes, which is amazing. It's pretty much a twenty-four hour job, especially in the spring.'

'We have that in common,' Tom said. 'Farming is much the same.'

'Thank you for taking the time to come over and visit,' Ruth said, hoping the colour wouldn't return to her face.

'I couldn't turn down your invite. I'm sorry I didn't reply. It's been madly busy and I wasn't sure I would be able to get away so I didn't want to say I would come and then not turn up.'

Now it was Ruth's turn to smile in amusement. Apparently she wasn't the only one who could get a little flustered.

'Trust me, I understand. I used to think that life as a veterinary nurse was full on, until I got into wildlife rescue and rehab.'

'I didn't realise you were a nurse.'

'I always knew this was what I wanted to do and it seemed the best way to gain the skills and experience. It means I can provide emergency care whilst waiting for the vet to arrive.'

'I'll bear your skills in mind, next time I need to give Colin his flea treatment. It really is a two-person job.'

'I thought you might bring him. I think Poppy is rather keen to see him again.'

Poppy had appeared out of the open door of the cottage and was now sniffing Tom's trousers.

'He's in the car but I wasn't sure about the rule on dogs,' Tom said.

'As long as he behaves, no problem.

Most of our animals are nocturnal so they're safely asleep in the sheds.'

'Well, in that case I'll go and get him. He hates being left in the car when there's something exciting going on.'

Ruth was busy serving tea and slices of cake. The visitors were being very generous paying for their tea but also making donations. It was the type of local support that Ruth had hoped would happen — not for the money but the interest and the willingness to get involved. It was the very essence of a sanctuary to have the people who lived nearby involved and engaged with what they were trying to do.

Ruth looked up at the sound of happy barking. Colin was straining on his lead as Poppy ran around him, yipping happily.

'Why don't you let Colin off in the paddock? They should be safe in there and then they can run around as much as they like.'

Ruth watched as Tom acknowledged her suggestion with a smile. Joe had obviously heard as he had the gate open and ready. Joe and Tom exchanged a few words and they didn't seem to be angry ones on Joe's part, which she took as a good sign.

A small girl tugged at Tom's arm and he knelt down so that he could speak to her on her level. Ruth couldn't make out the words but soon the little girl was in the paddock with the two dogs running around and screaming with laughter.

Within minutes all the children were in the paddock and the dogs were racing around chasing them and being chased.

Joe appeared in front of her and Ruth made him a cup of tea before cutting off a generous slice of lemon drizzle cake, which was Joe's favourite.

'Thanks, love, I'm parched.'

'I can't believe how well it's going,' Ruth said as Joe took a long slurp of tea.

'I always knew the locals would love it given half a chance.'

'We have lots of volunteers signed up and quite a few donations.'

Joe nodded and watched as Tom

climbed over the paddock fence and joined in with the kids and the dogs.

'It was good of Tom to come,' Ruth said. She didn't want to come right out with it and ask him what they talked about but she was hoping that Joe might give away a few clues.

She really liked Tom, but she trusted Joe's judgement and if he thought that there was more to Tom than she supposed, well she wasn't sure she wanted to risk the heartache of letting herself give in to her fluttering feelings.

Joe made a sort of grunt of acknowledgement.

'He's really good with the kids,' Ruth added, hoping that Joe might take the bait.

'Always was,' Joe said.

'Have you known him a long time?' Ruth knew that he had but was hoping playing dumb a little might get Joe talking.

'Since he was a nipper,' Joe said.

'How long did you work on the farm?'

'Nigh on twenty years,' Joe said seemingly lost in a memory, 'till Jeremy got his way.'

Ruth nodded. It wasn't much but a bit more of the puzzle. Perhaps Joe's opinion of Tom was clouded by his experiences and it was clear that Jeremy hadn't treated him well. If Tom was a young boy at the time maybe he hadn't known about what had happened.

Tom continued to play with the children until parents started to collect them to take them home. Ruth had shaken many hands and been told a lot that the place was wonderful.

Her mind had started to come with up new ideas and one of them was to give the children an opportunity to come and learn about the animals in a hands-on sort of way. She knew there were local groups like Brownies and thought that might be a good place to start.

'Penny for them?' Tom's voice startled Ruth out of her thoughts.

'I was just thinking about ways to get the children more involved,' Ruth said, glad that Tom hadn't caught her day-dreaming about him as he had before. 'I

51

thought I might contact the local leaders of Cubs and Brownies to see if they would be interested in a visit.'

'Good plan. I was thinking about doing something similar on the farm.'

Ruth looked at him carefully, wondering for a moment if he was making fun of her idea but his face just looked thoughtful.

'I loved being on the farm as a child and it's important to get the next generation involved. Someone will need to take over from us when we want to retire.'

Ruth laughed at the idea. To her, retirement was for people who didn't love their jobs. She couldn't imagine ever giving up the sanctuary but Tom was right. The more help they could get, the better.

'Perhaps we could do a joint day?' Ruth suggested. 'They could spend some time here in the afternoon and time with you in the morning. I guess those would be your busiest times?'

'It never seems to stop,' Tom said with a grin. 'Much like you, I suspect, but mornings would be good. Perhaps we could arrange to meet up and discuss it further? The village schools might be interested as well.'

Ruth smiled.

'Good. I could cook dinner?' she suggested, hoping she hadn't pushed the idea too far, too fast.

'Why don't you come to the farm and I'll cook?'

Ruth raised an eyebrow.

'I'll have you know that I'm a very good cook. My mum was very keen that her boys could look after themselves,' Tom said. 'And bring Poppy. She and Colin can have a run around the yard whilst we eat.'

'That sounds lovely,' Ruth said.

'Excellent, let's make it tomorrow night. If that works for you?'

'Perfect,' Ruth said.

Tom grinned back at her.

Joe appeared at the tea table.

'Last of the visitors have gone. Barbara and Sam are counting up the donations. We thought we should put a sign up in

53

the village to thank them for their generosity once we know how much has been raised.' Joe acknowledged Tom with a nod and Ruth thought he was thawing a little.

'It's been a great turn-out,' Tom said looking towards Joe, his gaze level.

'That it has,' Joe agreed, and Ruth was glad that he hadn't decided to air his views on who was trying to sabotage the sanctuary.

'Ruth and I were just discussing how to get the local kids more involved. They seemed keen to learn.'

'Aye, if you start 'em young enough,' Joe said.

'Well, we thought a joint venture between the farm and the sanctuary would be good. I'm going to cook dinner tomorrow evening so we can discuss the plans. Perhaps you could join us?'

Ruth bit the inside of her cheek to prevent her disappointment showing.

Maybe Tom didn't want to rush things and she couldn't disagree with that. Or maybe he thought that sorting things with Joe would make things easier for the sanctuary and that, she reminded her disappointed self, was the most important thing right now.

It could, of course, be that she and Tom were just destined to be friends and if that were the case, then she didn't want to reveal her feelings which might make things awkward if Tom didn't feel the same.

Joe was eyeing Tom carefully as if he was trying to read his mind.

'Now I don't think that would be a good idea, do you?' Joe said stiffly.

'Jeremy has his own place now on some land we brought at the edge of the farm, he won't be around tomorrow night.' Tom spoke the words carefully and Ruth knew she had another piece of the puzzle.

Whatever had happened between Joe and Jeremy, Tom knew at least some of it and she was determined to ask for the details when she had a chance.

Joe was clearly stuck to a certain extent by what had happened back then on the farm and unable to move on but if there was a way that Ruth could help him, then she would.

After all he had done for her, it really was the least she could do.

'Well, I don't know . . .' Joe said and he looked to Ruth. Ruth smiled and gave a little nod. 'OK, then. What time?' Joe said gruffly although Ruth was sure he was pleased.

'How about half five? I know it's early but then we can have a look round the place. You can see all that we've done.'

Joe was caught between the idea of going to see the place he had spent many happy years and the idea that it would be all 'new-fangled' as he would have put it, but he managed a curt nod.

'That would be lovely,' Ruth said.

Tom clipped Colin on to his lead.

'I'll see you both tomorrow, then,' Tom said and with a wave he was off, striding across the yard with Colin at his heels.

Ruth knew that Colin was too well trained to need a lead, he would have walked at Tom's heels whatever but at the same time she was grateful that Tom took the safety of her patients seriously enough not to want to risk it. The more she learned about Tom, the more perfect he appeared.

Dramatic Change of Plan

Joe was pacing the yard like he was waiting for his date to arrive. Ruth was peering out of the window and pulling a brush through her hair. The volunteers had arrived a little late and Ruth had spent some time making sure they were happy with what they were doing and so hadn't had much time to get ready.

She and Joe had agreed to meet at five, to give them plenty of time to walk over to the farm. Ruth only had a small compact mirror so she couldn't really check on her appearance.

Normally she wasn't bothered but she had a feeling that the farmhouse and its surroundings would be very grand and she didn't want to feel out of place.

Poppy was sitting inside the closed front door with a look of impatience on her face. Clearly she thought Ruth was fussing far too much.

'OK, OK,' Ruth said to Poppy, 'I'm coming.' Poppy stood up and nudged at the door. Ruth pulled it open and Poppy shot out to greet Joe. Ruth turned to pick up the bottle of wine that she was taking over as a gift.

'Hello, young lady. And how are you doing?' Joe asked Poppy, which made Ruth smile since he had only seen her a few hours before.

'Eager to run around with Colin again, I think,' Ruth said stepping out of the door and hoping she had made the right choice of clothes.

She was wearing a long, floaty skirt that sat just above her ankles so that she could wear her walking sandals. Ruth did not believe in style over comfort. She had a soft lemon cotton blouse that tied at her waist and a light waterproof over her arm that she could wear on the way home, should the weather be less than kind.

'Which way do you want to walk?' Ruth asked. 'Road or fields?'

'Fields, I reckon. It's not like Tom doesn't know we're coming.'

Ruth nodded, suspecting that Joe

wanted to take in the farm as they walked so that he could get used to how it looked now. Poppy barked and headed off in the right direct and not for the first time, Ruth was convinced that Poppy could understand every word that was said.

It was a warm spring evening and although the sun was setting in the distance, it was a pleasant walk. The right of way paths were clearly marked and Ruth and Joe made sure they stuck to them.

Joe seemed lost in memories so Ruth left him to it and gave herself the chance to think about everything that had happened in the last few months. It had been a complete whirlwind of events and she had worked every day for so long now she couldn't remember when she last had a day off. Not that she regretted a single day.

Her dream and her dad's dream was now real and even though she was living it, she still couldn't quite believe it. Her only regret was that her dad wasn't here to see it.

Ruth felt a sudden rush of loss, which

seemed to be how it was now. Most of the time she could think of him and just remember all the good times but now and then she felt like the air had been squeezed out of her lungs.

'You OK, love?' Joe asked softly.

Ruth knew she couldn't speak and so she just nodded. She felt Joe slip an arm around her shoulder and give her a quick squeeze. They both knew this dance well now and it was a comfort to have some-one who knew how you felt and knew when to speak and when to just offer a hug.

They walked on in silence for a bit as Poppy ran ahead and then ran back to check they were still there. This never failed to make Ruth smile. She leaned down and ruffled her ears.

'How does it feel to be back?' Ruth asked, hoping that Joe wouldn't mind the question.

'Fields are bigger — they've obviously done away with some of the hedgerows.'

Ruth nodded. That was not good news for wildlife but it had been the thing to do in recent times.

'But it's as beautiful as ever,' Joe said. 'Good quality soil up here, you see. Means if you rotate you can grow a variety of crops.'

Ruth and Joe walked on as Joe talked about farming and the dairy herd that old McMillan had had. They reached the edge of the farmyard and the Victorian farmhouse rose up before them.

It looked as though it had been extended but whoever had done the work had been sensitive to the original façade.

The front of the house was whitewashed and the windows were wooden with small glass panes. There was even a climbing rose that looked as if it had been there as long as the original farmhouse.

'As you remember?' Ruth asked.

'Not exactly,' Joe said. 'When I was here, we used to bring the young 'uns in to the kitchen to keep 'em warm in front of the range. Can't imagine them allowing that now it's all fancy.'

'There aren't any lights on inside,' Ruth said as they grew closer. She knocked on the front door, but there was no reply. Joe tried the door handle but it was locked.

'Was never locked, neither,' Joe said disapprovingly. 'Perhaps he forgot?'

Ruth didn't think that was likely. She scanned around the farmyard and spotted a soft glow of light from one of the barns. She pointed her finger and started to walk in that direction. Joe quickly fell into step beside her.

'Hello?' Ruth called but there was no answer. The bar gate to the barn was pulled shut and so instead of opening it, she climbed over.

'Poppy, wait,' she said and Poppy sat on her haunches, clearly desperate to follow Ruth but knowing she needed to stay.

Ruth jumped to the ground and stepped carefully though the straw.

'Hello?' she called again.

'First stall,' Tom's voice carried through the air.

'Is everything OK?' Ruth asked but as she turned to look into the first stall she knew that it wasn't. Tom was on his hands and knees beside Matilda the young highland calf. Matilda had a piece of barbed wire wrapped around her front leg and was making a high-pitched sound of distress.

'Somehow Matilda managed to find some barbed wire and get tangled in it,' Tom said pushing his hair back from his sweaty forehead. 'The vet is tied up and won't get here for several hours.'

Ruth moved into the stall and reached out a hand for Matilda. The calf's eyes were wide and she was panting.

'Let me call the vet who covers the sanctuary. I'm sure she'll come out,' Ruth said, pulling out her phone. Tom nodded.

'It's horrible to see her like this. I've tried the other farm vets but they're all on call outs. It's the season.'

Ruth nodded, then pressed the number and spoke quickly, explaining the situation.

'She'll be here in fifteen minutes,' Ruth said, hanging up. 'Do you have wire clippers? If we can get the barbed wire off, Matilda might be a bit more comfortable.'

Tom raised up a set that he had in the hay beside him.

'I've tried but I need help to hold her.' Ruth caught a glimpse of Tom's hands which were cut in several places and bleeding.

'We'll sort her. You go and sort your hands, lad,' Joe urged.

'Once Matilda's OK,' Tom said in the kind of voice that told Ruth there was no point in arguing.

Tom moved to Matilda's other side and started to whisper softly into the calf's ears. Joe moved to hold Matilda's leg so that Ruth could get to work. With Matilda relatively still, Ruth was able to remove the wire without injuring herself. She looked closely at the wound.

'It's not as bad as I first thought. I don't think it will need suturing — some surgical glue should do it,' Ruth said.

Tom nodded but he looked like he was having difficulty holding it together. Ruth recognised the expression. She had worn it herself many times, particularly when it was an animal she had developed a deep bond for.

'I just don't understand how it happened. The cattle were all in, safe for the night,' Tom said, shaking his head as he ran a hand down Matilda's side. She seemed to have calmed down a little.

'You know what young 'uns are like, lad, they look for and find mischief.'

Tom was shaking his head.

'But we don't use barbed wire anywhere on the farm. I won't have it. It's too easy for animals to get injured.'

Joe and Ruth exchanged glances as an uneasy feeling washed over them both.

'Well, we'll worry about that later. Let's get your hands washed, at least.'

Tom allowed himself to be led out of the stall and to the far wall where there was a tap and an old deep basin. Ruth turned on the water and Tom ran his hands underneath it.

66

'You came out of it worse than Matilda,' Ruth said. 'I think you're going to need to get checked out at the hospital.'

Tom looked at his hands as if he were seeing them for the first time.

'Once Matilda is OK,' he repeated.

'I'll take you now, you can't drive like that,' she insisted. Tom opened his mouth to protest but then taking in Ruth's expression, closed it again. 'And Joe can stay with Matilda.'

Tom nodded and then looked up as a set of headlights crossed the farmyard. Ruth walked out to meet Emily, the vet she had worked with for many years. Emily had experience of almost every animal there was farm, domestic and even a few exotics at the local zoo.

'Em, hi. This is Tom.'

Emily went to shake hands but then caught sight of Tom.

'I only do animals I'm afraid. For that you'll need a people doctor.'

'I'm going to take him to A and E,' Ruth said. 'Once Matilda is OK,' she added, looking at Tom.

Emily used glue to seal Matilda's wounds, gave an injection of pain relief and one of antibiotic before bandaging Matilda's leg with a blue waterproof bandage. She was efficient and gentle, all the while talking to Matilda who had calmed down considerably.

'I'd let her back in with her mum,' Emily said, standing up and patting Matilda on the side. 'They'll both be happier. The dressing will want changing in twenty-four hours and then I'd get your vet to review in forty-eight. If she loses her appetite or you're worried get a review sooner.'

'Thank you,' Tom said and he looked as if he had calmed considerably, 'for coming out and everything.'

'Animals don't keep office hours any more than sick people do and besides I've been doing it for more years than I care to count,' Emily said with a smile.

'But now you need to get yourself sorted out. Joe can keep an eye on Matilda and her mum.'

Ruth smiled. Emily had a way about

her that meant you just did what you told, it was part school teacher, part grandma.

'Thanks, Emily,' Ruth said, walking her out to the car. 'You are a life saver.'

'Never can ignore a call, you know that. I hear the sanctuary is up and running. I'm on the roster for next week so I'm sure I'll see you Monday.'

Emily gave Ruth a quick hug and then climbed back in her car and drove off.

'Right,' Ruth said to Tom, 'car keys?'

'I'm sure I can manage...' Tom started to say but one raised eyebrow from Ruth made him stop speaking. Like a chastised school boy, he reached carefully into his pocket and pulled out a set of keys. There were several vehicles to choose from but Tom gestured to an old Range Rover and they both climbed in.

It was Sunday night but the emergency department waiting room was almost full. There were children with bumped heads and people with arms in slings. Tom registered and then took a seat beside Ruth on one of the plastic chairs.

'It's about a two-hour wait, I'm afraid,' Tom said.

'No problem. I've rung Sam so they can stay on if we're back later than we thought.'

'Sorry about all this,' Tom said.

'Don't be daft. We'll pick up a takeaway on the way back,' Ruth said.

'I was supposed to be cooking dinner. I had it all ready but didn't get further than that.'

'You really don't have to explain that animals come first to a person who has sunk every penny into a wildlife sanctuary, you know,' Ruth said. 'I'm just glad Matilda is going to be OK.'

Tom nodded.

'I still can't work out how it happened.'

'It is strange but I'm sure it was just an accident.' But she couldn't help wondering if there was a connection between the nasty comments about her on the website and what had just happened.

She shook her head at the thought.

Writing anonymously was a bit different from actually harming an animal. No, it had to have been some kind of mistake.

'You heard what Joe said, young animals have a way of finding trouble. It could have been old wire left lying around that no-one had spotted,' Ruth said.

Tom shrugged but Ruth could tell that he was not convinced.

'Might be a good idea to do a check tomorrow, anywhere the cattle have been. If there's more out there you don't want Matilda finding it.'

Tom nodded, lost in thought.

Here's to Old Friends and New!

Ruth had been right and Tom had needed a few stitches but thankfully there was no serious damage to nerves or tendons. They left the emergency department with two bandaged hands and some antibiotics.

'How are you feeling?' Ruth asked as they climbed back into the battered Range Rover.

'A bit foolish and more than a little concerned.'

Ruth looked at him questioningly.

'I've been a farmer all my life but when I saw Matilda I panicked and just rushed in and tried to help. I should have called someone to help me remove the wire then I wouldn't have ended up like this.' Tom raised both hands to demonstrate.

'Look,' Ruth said, 'I work with animals every day like you and I'm a veterinary nurse. I'm a professional, too, but when it comes to Poppy or any other animal

I've become attached to I'm a wreck.

'It doesn't mean you're foolish. It just means you care.'

Ruth could feel Tom studying her face but she kept her focus on navigating her way out of the hospital car park.

'You're right, but in the farming community I'm often told it is a weakness.'

'Doesn't have to be. I mean, I suspect on some farms a bit more caring wouldn't go amiss.'

'True. My dad was a working farmer and did what needed to be done but he cared. He may not have shown it in public but in private, well let's just say you could tell that our animals were part of his family.'

'From what I've heard about your dad, he was the type of person you should want to be like and I wouldn't worry about what other people think.'

Ruth couldn't help but wonder if 'other people' included Jeremy who seemed to have a very business-like, if not totally detached, view of animals, as if all they were was a means to an end.

'He was a good man. I miss him,' Tom said, turning away to stare out of the window. Ruth didn't ask him any questions — she knew that look. The kind of look that told you the other person was lost in memories and it would be cruel to interrupt.

She also knew that Tom was likely having to fight to keep himself together and she didn't want to push him. Losing a parent was a unique type of pain and one that she suspected would never truly leave her.

They travelled in silence until they reached St Martin's, the nearest village to both the farm and the sanctuary and the one with the best fish and chip shop.

'I'll get it,' Tom said. 'It's the least I can do since I haven't managed to cook you dinner.'

Ruth was going to object but thought better of it.

'I brought wine, if you don't mind drinking it with chips?'

'Are you kidding? That's the best combination,' Tom said and he smiled. Ruth smiled back, glad that Tom seemed to be more like himself.

'Well, you buy and I'll carry. I'm not sure your hands will be up to much more.'

Back at the farm and Matilda was curled up asleep beside her mum. Joe was watching over them.

'Looks like Ruth was right and you needed to see a doctor,' Joe said wryly.

'A few stitches,' Tom said, looking at both his hands in their bright white bandages.

'Well, our other patient had a feed and is now fast asleep, as you can see.'

'Thanks for watching her,' Tom said, who seemed unable to tear his eyes away.

'She'll be fine now, lad. We'll check on her before we go but I think right now, if my nose is right, we have some dinner to eat.'

The large kitchen had obviously been modernised but it still had the right feeling. The huge wood-burning stove meant that the room was warm and cosy.

Poppy and Colin were curled up

together in one basket, right by the fire but leaped up to greet them when they opened the door. Colin sniffed at Tom's bandaged hands and whimpered so Tom knelt down and wrapped his arms around his dog's neck.

'I'm fine, boy, and so is Matilda.' Colin licked Tom's nose, greeted the others and then returned to his basket, leaving room for Poppy.

The large wooden table, long enough to seat at least ten people, looked like the only thing that hadn't been updated.

'Can't believe you kept this,' Joe said, taking a seat on the long wooden bench and running his hands over the surface. 'Lots of memories here.'

'I couldn't bear to part with it. The water pipes burst one winter and flooded the whole place so it all needed redoing but I saved the flagstones and the table.'

Joe nodded in appreciation. Since the table was already laid, Ruth handed around the wrapped parcels of fish and chips and then went in search of ketchup in the large fridge freezer. Joe had put her bottle of wine in there too, so she pulled it out and filled everyone's glass.

'A toast, I think?' Tom said, gingerly holding his glass in one hand.

'How about to neighbours?' Ruth said. They all raised their glasses and clinked them together.

'And old friends and new,' Tom said, looking first to Joe and then Ruth. They clinked glasses again and Ruth could see Joe colour a little.

'It's about time you were back round this table, where you belong,' Tom said.

Joe cleared his throat and nodded, before tucking into his piece of cod, which both Ruth and Tom took to mean he wasn't able to speak right now.

Once they had all started to eat, the conversation flowed. Tom told them about how the farm had changed since his father had died and Joe came out of his shell and joined in.

Ruth was collecting up the plates thinking about washing up when she realised that Tom had a dishwasher, so instead started to load that, knowing that Tom needed to keep his bandages clean and dry.

'How are you going to manage, lad, with your hands like that?' Joe asked.

Tom shrugged.

'I have some labourers.'

Ruth knew that Joe was dying to get back out on the farm and do some work but she also knew that Jeremy might cause a problem.

'Well, we have a roster of volunteers so I can manage at the sanctuary for a few days, Joe, so feel free to help out,' Ruth said.

Joe looked at Tom and they seemed to have a silent conversation. Ruth knew it was about Jeremy but somehow neither of them seemed to need to voice out loud what that meant.

'It's still my farm, Joe,' Tom said the words quietly, 'so if you would be happy to help, I'd appreciate it. Particularly with the Highland herd, as I do all their care.'

'Righto,' Joe said gruffly but everyone knew that he was very happy to have the chance to work with the herd again. 'In that case, we should be going. It's gone ten and I'll be back at five.'

'Thanks, Joe,' Tom said, offering out his hand. Joe looked at it and grinned.

'You are going to have to keep your hands clean for once. Your fingernails were the bane of your mother's life.' Joe's eyes sparkled at the memory and Tom laughed.

Ruth couldn't quite believe that an evening that had started so badly could finish so well.

'I'll pop over tomorrow and change your bandages,' Ruth said, 'as long as you don't mind me being a veterinary nurse rather than a people nurse? Bandaging is much the same, although animals tend to be more awkward patients.'

'I don't want to bother you. I know you're busy.'

'Friends, remember?' Ruth said, reminding Tom of his toast.

'Then that would be great,' Tom said, walking them to the door. 'But remember that works both ways.

'Friends and neighbours help each other out, so if you need anything you only have to ask.'

Ruth smiled and whistled at Poppy, who seemed reluctant to leave both her warm spot and her companion.

'Come on, Pops,' Ruth said.

'Not to worry, Poppy, I think we will be seeing a lot more of each other from now on.' Tom's eyes sought out Ruth's and for the first time that evening Ruth wondered if Tom shared her feelings, that maybe there was more between them than just a possible friendship.

* * *

Ruth found it hard to concentrate the next day, partly because she had been up early to do the baby bird rota and partly because her mind seemed to insist on replaying the dinner she had last night with Tom and Joe.

It could hardly be classed as romantic since she and Tom were not alone but somehow it made her heart skip more

80

than if they had been. If Tom was prepared to be so open about his feelings then Ruth was sure she wasn't imagining them.

She had texted Tom first thing to suggest she head over to the farm around five to change his bandages, since she was sure that they would be dirty from a day's work, however much Joe helped out.

Tom had texted back that would be great and he would make sure he had a cuppa on standby and so all Ruth could do was try not to look at her watch more than once every 10 minutes and get on with the large list of jobs there was to do every day when you cared for animals.

Without Joe, Ruth had more than enough to do and so was almost surprised when her phone beeped to tell her it was half four and time to get cleaned up and walk over to the farm. Barbara had arrived with a fresh bunch of volunteers and so Ruth had a few hours free.

'Back to the farm, are you?' Barbara asked, faking innocence when Ruth went to tell her she was off.

Ruth grinned. There was no point hiding it. She was excited to see Tom again and it felt like her life, the one she had worked so hard to create, was finally starting to come together.

To find a man who shared her passion for the countryside and animals hadn't seemed possible up till now, but that was before she met Tom.

Poppy ran ahead of her as they crossed the fields. Ruth had changed out of her dirty work jeans and into a new pair and pulled on a clean black T-shirt.

She was going over to change bandages and didn't want to look like she had dressed up for the occasion. Poppy heard the noise before she did and stopped in her tracks. Her hackles rose and she didn't look like she wanted to walk any further.

'What is it?' Ruth asked but then she could make out the raised voices. She leaned down to stroke Poppy who looked up questioningly.

'We better go and see what's going on,'

Ruth said and Poppy fell into step beside her, no longer happy to run ahead.

They reached the large farmyard and Ruth tried to take in the scene. Jeremy was standing beside one of the work trucks which had a pile of rubbish in the back, and was yelling at Joe. Joe was standing his ground and yelling back.

Tom was watching what was going on as if he didn't know what to do. He saw Ruth approach and looked at her and then turned away. Ruth stopped, too, wondering if that was Tom's way of telling her not to get involved.

'You're telling me that all this,' Jeremy yelled, gesturing at the load on the back of the truck, 'is nothing to do with that wretched sanctuary of yours?'

'I'm telling you that Ruth and I took all of the waste to the tip.' Joe's voice was quieter but steely none the less. 'And you accusing us of anything different is slander!'

Searching for the Enemy

Ruth could not believe what she was hearing and knew that there had to be some kind of mistake. Jeremy and Joe were glaring at each, seemingly at a stalemate.

'Fly tipping is an offence, you know,' Jeremy said although whether he was talking to Joe and Ruth or Tom, Ruth wasn't sure.

'What exactly is going on?' Ruth demanded, looking at Tom.

'Jeremy has found the source of the barbed wire. There's a pile of rubbish containing broken up wood, chicken wire and other things on the border between our two properties.'

'That's terrible,' Ruth said, feeling outraged that anyone would do that — it was the height of laziness — not to mention illegal and damaging to the environment. 'I understand that feelings run high about stuff like this but what's it got to do with us?'

Tom's face was unreadable as if he had pulled up the shutters and wasn't prepared to give anything away.

'Because there's a sign that belonged to the previous owner of your so-called sanctuary,' Jeremy spat out. 'Along with the barbed wire that nearly killed our prize calf.'

Ruth felt some of the colour drain from her face. It wasn't possible. She and Joe had taken every last piece of rubbish to the tip and George, the previous owner, had barely been able to walk out of the cottage.

The idea that he could have loaded up a van and driven the rubbish before dumping it was absurd. Surely Tom had to see that.

She turned to look at him again, opening her mouth to point out the ridiculousness but then she saw his face and this time he was giving something away. It was just a shadow, a flicker even, but there was doubt. And Ruth felt like she had been punched in the stomach.

'I'm telling you, we took every last

piece to the tip and disposed of it correctly.'

'Then how do you explain how it got there?' Jeremy threw back the words and Ruth was starting to get concerned that at some point someone might actually throw a physical punch.

'I can't tell you how but I can tell you it wasn't us. The countryside — not to mention the wildlife — is very too important to us. We would never . . .'

Ruth was cut off by Jeremy.

'Apparently your concern is limited to wild vermin and not cattle.'

Ruth glared at him.

'If that were true then why would we have helped Tom with Matilda?'

'Because you were worried that you would get found out. It's one thing to dump rubbish, that's a small fine but if you caused injury to prize cattle it could cost you thousands of pounds,' Jeremy said and Ruth could see that Tom was considering the words.

'And I have no doubt that you felt some guilt — after all, Tom has been supporting your little venture.'

Ruth knew in that moment that this was an argument she couldn't win. Jeremy had made up his mind all she could hope to do was talk to Tom and make him see how ridiculous the accusation was.

'I think perhaps you should leave,' Tom said softly. Ruth didn't know what to say. How could he believe that she would do such a thing?

She was foolish to think that he would know her well enough to know that it was a ridiculous accusation. It was clear that nothing was going to change his mind.

'Joe, let's go. It's clear we're no longer welcome.'

Joe moved to her side and Ruth called Poppy and together they walked out on to the lane. They didn't need to speak to each other to say that crossing Tom's fields was no longer an option. They walked away in silence.

Ruth desperately wanted to look round to see if there was a flicker of hope in Tom's expression, that perhaps there was some sign that he had considered her words but she didn't think she could bear to see his doubt one more time.

The sun was starting to set but they could still see well enough to walk safely and besides there was hardly any traffic this far out of the village.

'That man is a liar,' Joe finally said, through gritted teeth.

'He's wrong about us, Joe, but someone put that rubbish on their land,' Ruth said. She had forced her mind away from the look on Tom's face to trying to work out exactly what was going on.

'Maybe whoever wrote the anonymous messages on the website? Perhaps this is the next step in their campaign against the sanctuary.'

This thought was almost as bad as the idea of losing Tom as a friend and Ruth felt a sense of helplessness wash over her. It simply wasn't fair. She didn't know who her enemy was and so there was no way to defend herself from the attack.

'I'm telling you it's Jeremy. I've seen him do this before.'

'Joe, I'm not saying I like the man but that's a serious allegation and we have no proof. Besides, why would he want to discredit us like that?'

'As I told you before, Ruthie, he wants the land,' Joe said darkly.

But Ruth still couldn't see that was enough of a motivation for Jeremy to do what Joe was suggesting. It just didn't make sense to her.

'He was behind my having to leave,' Joe said.

'I guessed as much, Joe, but you've never told me what happened.'

'That's because I could never prove it, Ruthie. Some stuff went missing from the farm. Not big stuff, mind, just the odd thing here and there. And on my word I never touched it,' Joe said, looking to Ruth to gauge her reaction.

'No need to convince me, Joe. I trust you implicitly.'

Joe nodded and there was a look of relief on his face.

'But Jeremy managed to convince old man McMillan that it was me. He didn't want to let me go, I'd worked with him for years but in the end he felt he had no choice. Jeremy was pushing him to get the police involved and McMillan said that if he did, my reputation would be ruined.

'Just the idea that I was being investigated would get the gossips going and to some of them it wouldn't matter that I would be found innocent so in the end I agreed to leave.'

It was darker now and Ruth couldn't make out Joe's face but she could hear the pain and sorrow in his voice.

'I saw the same doubt in McMillan's eyes as I did in Tom's today. Nearly killed me back then.'

'I'm so sorry, Joe. I don't really know what to say.'

'Well, as Peggy said, at least my reputation was intact and I knew the truth.'

'Not much of a consolation at losing your job,' Ruth said, starting to wonder if Joe was right about Jeremy but feeling like if he was there was lots of pieces of the puzzle still missing.

'No, but I could walk around with my head held high, lass, and that means something to a man. And besides, that got me into working with the charity, so I count myself lucky.'

'I'm sorry about the circumstances but I could have never have pulled the sanctuary together without you.'

'If you carry on like that, Ruthie, you'll make this old man blush.'

'Well, one thing's for sure, whoever is behind this, whether it's Jeremy or someone else, they aren't going to get away with it. We've worked too hard for too long to let them damage our reputation.'

'Too right, Ruthie. Anything you need from me, just ask.'

Ruth nodded, even though she knew that Joe couldn't see much of her now. They turned into the drive way and walked into the yard.

'Do you need any more help this evening?' Joe asked.

'No, I'll be fine. We have fewer baby birds on round the clock so I can manage. You go off home.'

'I'll be back bright and early,' he said before leaning in to give Ruth a quick hug. 'And try not to worry. We aren't going to let some bully bring us down.'

Ruth stayed and waved Joe off in his old van before turning to walk into the bird shed. Ruth had phoned the volunteers and told them they were on the way and that they could go, she was also sorry that she was so late back.

She did the rounds with the birds, some of which were starting to fledge and could go a little longer without needing food. The smaller, younger ones were all in one incubator and she unplugged it and carried it back to the cottage.

It was much warmer and more comfortable in there, especially if she was on her own and she could try to get a bit of sleep in between feeds.

There was not much sleep to be had as Ruth tried to work out who was behind the mean tricks that were being played on her, with serious consequences.

She pulled out a pen and paper and wrote down everything that had happened and then tried to come up with a list of names of who it could be.

The problem was, Ruth couldn't imagine who would have it in for the sanctuary enough to go to such lengths. Anonymous comments were one thing, taking seconds to write, but getting rubbish back from the tip and then dumping it on Tom's land — that took effort and planning. It just didn't make sense.

The only person Ruth could think of was Jeremy. He certainly seemed to have pulled some dirty tricks in the past but she could see what his motive would be this time.

The sanctuary was a small piece of land, particularly in comparison to McMillan's, and beside that she couldn't see why they needed it, since they had engulfed the only other small farms around. It just didn't seem enough for Jeremy to bother with.

She wanted to go and speak to Tom but she knew she had nothing new to say. What she needed was some sort of proof that would show she wasn't involved.

It irked her that she needed to prove herself to him and she wondered what effect his doubt would have on their friendship, let alone anything more, but right now she couldn't bear for him to think badly of her.

It wasn't fair and it wasn't right — not to mention the fact that she didn't want anyone thinking badly of the sanctuary. Their work was too important to be undermined like this.

Ruth looked again at all the things that had happened. One place she could go was back to the tip to see if they remembered anything. Hopefully they would remember her and Joe in the old van that had the sanctuary name painted on the side along with transfers of badgers and hedgehogs. If they did, maybe she could get them to speak up for her.

Maybe they would even know who might have taken the rubbish back and that would give her a first piece of evidence. Assuming the staff at the tip weren't involved.

Ruth shook her head. No, she wasn't

going to start pointing fingers at people who were likely as innocent as she was. Instead she would get solid proof and then maybe they could try to work out who was really behind it all.

No Further Forward

Joe was in early as usual, and although Ruth had barely slept she felt full of energy and purpose. She had checked the rota and Sam was due in later, so once she and Joe had completed the morning rounds of feeding, cleaning out and medical checks, she would be free to drive up to the tip and ask the staff if they had any information.

'You look like you haven't slept much,' Joe said taking in the dark circles under her eyes. 'Birds or worries?' he asked.

Ruth smiled.

'Birds a little bit, but I've also been working on a plan.'

Joe raised an eyebrow but said nothing, which Ruth took as a sign that she could continue.

'Well, we know the rubbish didn't come from us and that we took every last piece of the tip.' Joe nodded but didn't seem to make the same connections as Ruth had. 'So I thought I would go and speak to the staff up there. See if anyone remembers us taking the rubbish up there.'

Joe looked thoughtful.

'That would help, but I don't suppose they will remember exactly what we took. Jeremy will just say that we took some stuff to the tip and dumped the rest.'

'I thought of that, but I was also going to ask if they could remember anyone else coming up to the tip and acting suspiciously. Surely they would notice if someone was taking stuff away from the tip.'

Joe's face twitched and he managed a little smile.

'I expect they would. You can buy stuff up there, of course, but we put everything in the bins, not in the shed for resale.'

'Exactly,' Ruth said, her eyes flashing with triumph. She had felt so helpless yesterday but now she felt like she was taking back some control. 'So I thought once Sam arrived I could take a little trip.'

'I'll come, too. I've known Billy up

there for years and we can trust his word.'

The morning was busier than expected as a couple had found an injured fox cub which looked as though it had been bitten and the wound was infected.

With the fox cub settled and all the animals sorted, Joe and Ruth climbed in the sanctuary van and headed for the tip. It was a Tuesday morning in term time and so there were only a few other people there. Ruth pulled the van into one of the free spots and climbed out.

Joe scanned the members of staff and spotted Billy standing near the portacabin that functioned as the office, talking to a much younger lad. He caught sight of Joe and raised and arm in welcome.

'Billy, how's things?' Joe asked, shaking the outstretched hand.

'Oh, you know, not so bad,' Billy said with a smile that revealed a few missing teeth.

'This is Ruth — she's the one who set up the sanctuary near the McMillan farms.'

'Old George's place,' Billy said with a

smile at Ruth. 'I know I wasn't the only one to be glad it stayed a smallholding.'

Billy looked from Ruth to Joe. Now she was here, Ruth wasn't quite sure how to start the conversation.

'Bill, we've been having some bother with you-know-who,' Joe said and Ruth thought Billy might not know who he was referring to but Billy cottoned on immediately.

'Aye well, there's no real surprise there, is there?' Billy answered. 'What does he claim you've done this time?'

'Fly tipping,' Ruth said. 'There's a pile of rubbish on the border between our properties and some of it obviously belonged to old George. There's even the signpost for the old smallholding.'

Billy nodded.

'But we brought every last bit of here, mate,' Joe said.

'I remember you coming back and forth that's for sure,' Billy said. 'Old George is a good man but he was a bit of a hoarder.' Billy looked thoughtful. 'So you'll be wanting to know how waste from here got back to the farm?'

Joe nodded and Ruth waited, feeling her heart beating in her chest, hoping that Billy was about to provide them with some evidence that she could take back to Tom.

'Not on my watch,' Billy said, 'but then I'm not here every day any more.' Billy looked beyond them to scan the staff working across the site.

'But then young Terry is keen as mustard and has been known to sell a few bits on the side, like.

'Terry!' Billy yelled so loud that Ruth thought her eardrum might burst. A young, skinny lad with a serious case of teen acne and a bright fluorescent shirt, which did nothing for his complexion, ran over.

'You're not in trouble, lad, I just want to ask you if you've made any off the books sales recently.'

Terry looked at Ruth and Joe and then back to Billy, as if trying to judge who they were and how much trouble he was in, despite Billy's words.

'Speak up, lad, I promise there'll be no trouble.'

'A couple of customers wanted a few bits, nothing dangerous, so I didn't see the 'arm.'

'Did any of 'em take stuff that we brought?' Joe asked, gesturing to the sanctuary van which, with its detail, was fairly memorable.

Terry nodded reluctantly.

'Were they from McMillan's?' Joe asked.

'No, guv. Just some young guy, said he was into recycling and thought he could make use of some of the wire and that.' Terry looked to Billy, checking on his reaction.

'Righto, son, back to work.'

'Don't suppose you have CCTV?' Ruth asked, feeling some of the earlier hope fade a little.

Billy snorted.

'Council won't even buy us tea, lass, no chance of anything that fancy, but I'll ask around and see if anyone else can give us any more detail. I'll call you if I find anything.'

'Thanks, mate,' Joe said holding out his hand and shaking Billy's.

Joe and Ruth climbed back into the van.

'Well, at least we can tell Tom that we have a witness to someone taking our rubbish from the tip.'

Joe gave her a look which suggested he didn't think that would help much and Ruth was a little worried he might be right.

'It's a pity we don't have a registration. We could have gone to the police.'

'And told 'em what, Ruthie? It ain't a crime to buy rubbish from the tip.'

'So much for my plan,' Ruth said miserably, pulling the van out on to the road.

'Don't be giving up just yet. Billy may still come through for us.'

Ruth's mobile rang and Joe answered it.

'Just what you need, a distraction,' Joe said after he had hung up. 'Farm over Beddington way has a young doe caught in a fence.'

By the time Joe and Ruth got back to the sanctuary they were tired, sweaty and very muddy. They had freed the doe, who had no injuries.

They'd been able to release her straight away but not before they had both been covered in mud and other things they preferred not to think about. The deer had managed to get stuck in a fence near to the pigs wallowing area.

Still, Ruth felt in better spirits. If nothing else she was doing what she set out to do and helping wildlife in distress.

She pulled the van into the yard with her mind fixed on the cup of tea she was going to make as soon as she could. In the yard was the same old motor that Ruth had driven Tom to the hospital in, a few nights before.

She couldn't see Tom but Poppy and Colin were racing around the yard together, taking it in turns to chase each other.

Ruth climbed out of the van and caught a glimpse of herself in the side mirror. Her hair was a mess, wild with bits of straw sticking out at angles and one look down at her clothes and she knew she looked like she had been rolling around in mud.

'What does he want?' Joe said, looking towards the bird shed and seeing Tom through the window.

'Don't know,' Ruth said.

She couldn't bear to say out loud that she hoped he had come to apologise, to say that he had thought it through and was now sure she and Joe couldn't have been involved.

What if he hadn't? What if he had come to say that he had called in the police? She didn't think she could take it.

'I dying for a cuppa. Do you want one?' Joe asked.

'Please,' Ruth said. 'You know where everything is in the cottage.'

'Aye,' Joe said before sending another dark look in Tom's direction and walking off to the cottage.

Ruth thought she should have asked Joe to make one for Tom, too, but wasn't sure she wanted him to stay that long, if he had come to tell her bad news.

The outer door to the bird shed opened and Tom stepped out.

'Hi, Ruth,' he said. He sounded as if he wasn't sure what sort of reception he might receive and Ruth felt OK about that. He had not two days ago accused her of a crime after all.

'Tom, I wasn't expecting to see you,' Ruth said, keeping her voice neutral. She didn't want to give away the fact that she had hoped he would come over. Come over and beg forgiveness.

'I was just helping Sam out whilst I was waiting. I can't believe how much the birds have grown in such a short space of time.'

Ruth nodded.

'Some of them will be fully fledged soon then we can get them in the aviary and start preparing them for release.' Ruth was pretty sure he hadn't come over to discuss the welfare of baby birds and hoped that the fact he didn't seem to want to get to the point, wasn't bad news.

'How's Matilda?' she asked, when Tom didn't appear to want to fill the silence.

'Really good. My vet came this morning and said it's all healing up and we should be able to ditch the bandages in a week or so.'

'That's good to hear,' Ruth said. There was silence again. 'And how about you?' Ruth asked, gesturing to Tom's hands and wondering at how things could be so awkward now.

'Not too bad. Stitches out on Friday and then I'll just need to keep them covered until they dry out.'

Ruth nodded. She was running out of things to ask when Joe appeared bearing two steaming mugs. He glared at Tom and then handed a mug to Ruth.

'I'll be down fixing the water trough in the paddock, Ruthie, if you need me.'

'Thanks, Joe,' she said and let herself waste a few seconds watching him go and taking a sip of hot tea. It really was Tom's turn to speak and she wasn't about to fill the silence again.

'I wanted to talk to you, if that's OK?'

106

Tom asked. Ruth looked at him and nodded and then led the way to the bench outside the cottage. Colin and Poppy ran up and gave them an enthusiastic greeting before charging off in the direction of Joe and the paddock.

'They really do like each other,' Tom observed and Ruth sighed. 'Sorry. I'm procrastinating.'

Ruth took a sip of tea and said nothing. Since she agreed with him there was no point.

'I wanted to say that I was sorry about yesterday.'

Ruth felt some of the tension leave her shoulders.

'Thank you.'

'Jeremy shouldn't have spoken to you like that. That's not how neighbours should speak to each other if they have a problem.'

'A problem?' Ruth said raising a challenging eyebrow and forgetting her tea for a moment. 'I don't know how many more times I can tell you, Tom, but we didn't dump that rubbish.'

'Look, I'm sure you didn't personally but perhaps someone who was helping you out took a short cut.

'It doesn't matter now, the rubbish has been dealt with and Matilda is on the mend. I don't want it to affect our friendship.' Tom looked at her and smiled.

The kind of smile that said all was forgiven but that was the last thing Ruth was looking for.

'It matters to me, Tom,' Ruth said, standing up. 'It matters that you don't believe me when I tell you something. That's not the basis for a friendship.

'You say all is forgiven but in saying that you're showing you don't believe what I say, that you have something to forgive me for.'

Tom looked a confused as if this wasn't playing out how he had imagined it in his head.

'I went to the tip today to see if I could find out how the rubbish we took there ended up on your land. One of the staff was paid some money to allow a young lad to take it away. He said he was going to reuse it but that clearly wasn't the case.'

Tom had stood up now and was shaking his head.

'So you're saying this mysterious person brought your rubbish to dump it on my farm? Come on, Ruth, that's a bit far-fetched. Can't we just agree that it's over and move on?'

'Not while you still think I had something to do with it.' Ruth could feel her voice get louder but she didn't seem to be able to calm down. 'I'm passionate about the countryside and I would never dump rubbish.

'The fact that you think I might have let someone do that on my behalf, just to cut a few corners, is outrageous and proves that you don't know me at all.'

The sentence had come out all in one breath, Ruth's anger was starting to unfold and she knew she was in danger of saying something she might later regret.

Tom whistled and Colin appeared at his side.

'I came here to mend fences, Ruth, but it's clear to me that you aren't interested.'

'There are no fences to mend since I had nothing to do with it. I was expecting you to come here and apologise to me for even thinking I could do something like that.'

Tom looked at her and all warmth was gone from his face. His cheeks coloured a little but he looked at her coldly.

'You expect me to believe that someone actually went to the tip to buy your rubbish? For what purpose? You must realise how ridiculous that sounds.'

'It's not ridiculous if someone has some sort of vendetta against me and the sanctuary.'

Tom laughed harshly.

'Ruth, really! Why on earth would anyone want to do that?'

'Why don't you ask Jeremy?' Ruth spat the words out. She hadn't meant to say anything about Jeremy. It wasn't as if they had any actual proof it was him but right now he was the only person that

Ruth could think would be involved and she was too angry to keep her own counsel about it.

Tom looked as if he had been slapped.

'That's your answer to all this? To try to smear a good man's reputation? A man who has been like a father to me?'

Ruth didn't know what to say. She couldn't believe that everything had spiralled so quickly into this.

'Tom, let's . . .' But she didn't get any further because without saying another word, Tom was striding away to his car.

False Statement

'Hey,' Joe said, pulling Ruth into his arms. She was crying bitter tears now. Whoever was playing dirty tricks on her had now cost her a friendship. A friendship she had thought might become more. They were achieving their goals of ruining her reputation, too.

Joe said nothing, just rubbed her back, as her dad would have done if he had been there. Thoughts of her dad made the tears flow faster and so Joe walked her to the bench and sat them both down. He held her until she had cried herself out.

'There now, lass,' he said softly as she moved to sit up straight. He brushed some hair from her face and smiled gently.

'He still thinks it was us, Joe. He thought our theory was crazy.'

Joe nodded.

'I heard.'

'Whoever is doing this is getting exactly

what they want. Now Tom thinks that not only did I let rubbish be dumped on his land but I also made up a story to cover it up.'

'What Tom believes is up to him. We know the truth.'

'That won't do me much good if he tells other people and they start to believe it, too. No-one is going to help out at a wildlife sanctuary if they think we purposely do things to damage the environment.'

'Anyone who knows you won't believe it, lass,' Joe said sternly.

'But I thought Tom knew me and look what just happened!' Ruth could feel the angry, hurt tears start to build in her eyes but she brushed them away with a frustrated hand.

'No-one else has Jeremy whispering poison in their ears,' Joe said.

'Joe, I know you don't like the man but it's not like we have any evidence to prove he's involved.'

'Aye, but we will. We just have to keep watch for it. He'll make a mistake, you mark my words — and when he does we'll be ready.'

'Will that be before or after the public lose all faith in us?' Ruth asked miserably.

'We aren't going to let him destroy this place,' Joe said firmly.

'And that starts with you having a bit of faith in us. We worked too hard to get his place set up and we are already achieving great things. No farm owner wannabe is going to take that from us, you hear?'

Ruth managed a watery smile at Joe's passionate speech. He usually didn't say all that much so this was even more of a surprise. She reached out and squeezed his hand.

'And it's not just you and me, lass. We have an army of volunteers who believe in what we are doing here. They won't be letting someone tear it down.'

Ruth nodded as Poppy rested her head in her lap. Ruth scratched Poppy behind her ears.

'You're right. I'm sorry. I just got a little overwhelmed.'

'Now's time to pick yourself up and get back to the fight,' Joe said.

Ruth nodded and got to her feet.

'About time we checked in on the foxes,' Ruth said, turning to look at Joe.

'That's the Ruthie I know.'

★　★　★

A few days later and Joe checked in with Billy, who had nothing to report. The young lad who had brought the rubbish was not a familiar face and they hadn't seen him since. No-one could remember what make of vehicle he was driving, only that it was a pale coloured hatchback.

Ruth had tried to hide her disappointment when Joe told her the news. It had seemed to be the last bit of hope, that they might be able to track the young lad down and ask him what he was doing and why.

Still, the sanctuary had been busy and Ruth hadn't had much opportunity to think about what had happened. She hadn't seen or heard from Tom but then she wasn't really surprised by that since there really wasn't anything else to say.

'Ruth, you better come look at this.' Joe's voice cut through Ruth's musings and she carefully lowered the lid to the hedgehog den and made sure the latch was firmly shut.

'What's up?' Ruth asked, her mind considering the possibilities of animals that might have taken a turn for the worse or possible rescue scenarios that might have been called in. They were almost full so she wasn't quite sure where they would put a new arrival but they always found space and never turned an animal away.

One look at Joe's face and she knew it was none of the options she had considered.

'What now?' she asked as she walked over to Joe and Sam who were standing close together and looking at something.

'I can hardly bear to show you this, Ruth,' Sam said before reluctantly hold-

116

ing out a piece of paper. 'One of the kids saw it on a lamppost and thought you would want to know about it.'

Ruth took the piece of paper, which seemed to be some kind of computer generated flyer.

It read: 'More evidence that the so called Wildlife Sanctuary is just a money-making sham!' Written in bold capital letters it was hard to miss. 'Want to know where your money is really going? Then log on to the community website Wednesday 24th at 7 p.m., for damning evidence!'

Ruth read the flyer several times more to give herself time to process the words.

'Where did they find it?' she asked.

'I sent the boys out,' Sam said grimly, 'and they found over twenty all around the village. They've taken them all down but old grumpy in the post office said they'd been put up the night before.'

'So plenty of folks will have seen them,' Joe said, his voice low but his anger obvious.

'I just heard,' Barbara said, coming

out of the bird shed. 'But it's nonsense, what possible evidence could he have?'

'I'm not sure he needs any. He could make anything up and people might still start to doubt what we are doing here.'

'Well, it isn't the books,' Sam said firmly. 'And I'm happy go ahead and get an independent review.' Ruth tried a smile. It wasn't really something she could afford and there was no way she was using donated money for that.

'I'm not sure I can afford . . .' she started to say but Sam held up her hand.

'I can call in a favour.'

'But if that somehow got out, it wouldn't help,' Ruth pointed out, squeezing Sam's arm to show she was thankful for the offer.

'Maybe we need to wait and see what he has to say? Maybe it will be nothing,' Barbara added hopefully.

Ruth nodded.

'Barbara's right. Let's just wait and see. It's possible he is just bluffing.'

Everyone exchanged glances, doing

their best to look positive but Ruth knew they were all thinking the same thing. Why would a person put out flyers if he had nothing to share?

'Ruthie's right, there's nowt we can do right now but get back to work,' Joe said and they all turned away, back to their tasks.

Ruth walked away, racking her brains for anything that she had done recently that could be misconstrued and could come up with nothing. She hadn't made any big personal purchases. Even the idea of it was laughable. She bought all her clothes from charity shops and food from the cheapest supermarket. Her life was the very definition of frugal living so what could this person think they have against her? She shook her head, she wasn't going to come up with any answers until seven o'clock and until then all she could do was work.

★ ★ ★

At ten to seven, Joe, Barbara, Sam and Ruth were all huddled around the small kitchen table in Ruth's cottage.

Ruth had logged on to the community website and clicked on to the comments section. Nobody had made any sort of comment since the night before when a villager had reported some young people hanging around in the wood behind their property.

All they could do was stare at the computer and wait for the clock to tick around to seven. Seven o'clock arrived and passed and Ruth was just about to suggest that whoever had made the posters was just bluffing when there was a beep and a new message appeared on screen.

'What the sanctuary doesn't want you to know!' was the message and alongside it was an image. The image was of a bank statement — an electronic one that had all Ruth's details on it and a long list of financial deposits. They all stared at the screen. Ruth wasn't sure what she had expected but definitely not this.

'That's not my bank statement,' she said out loud, even though she knew everyone agreed with her. 'I bank with Midland Trust.'

'And the sanctuary account is with Bishops,' Sam said.

'It's clearly a fake,' Barbara said. 'No-one is going to believe that. I mean how would he have got hold of it, without breaking the law?'

'I think the more important question is why is he doing this?' Ruth asked.

'We know who it is — maybe it's time we confronted him.'

'We have no evidence,' Sam said sternly, 'and if we are wrong we will only make things worse for Ruth and the sanctuary. No — we need to find out who is behind this and then confront them with proof.'

'But how?' Joe said gruffly. Clearly he was relishing the idea of going over to McMillan's and having it out with Jeremy.

'I'm going to go back to the website and see if I can track down where the message is coming from,' Sam said.

'You know how to do that?' Ruth asked.

'No — but I know a kid who does,' Sam said. She nodded at them all and then stood up before walking to the door. 'I'll let you know what I find out.'

'I honestly don't think anyone will believe it,' Barbara said kindly. 'They'll see it for what it is, a mean trick.'

'I just can't think why anyone would want to do this to the sanctuary. We save wildlife, for goodness sake. Who can object to that?' Ruth didn't look at Joe as she knew exactly what he would say.

'No-one,' Barbara said firmly. 'Maybe it is just some kids playing a game and not realising how much trouble they are causing.'

Ruth nodded. That would be easier to take than someone with a genuine vendetta but there was still a part of her that couldn't believe that. It felt like someone had a real issue with her and the sanctuary, she just couldn't figure who that might be.

Since there wasn't much more to say or do, Joe took Barbara home, promising to be back first thing in the morning. Ruth did her final checks on all the animals and then returned to the cottage. She ought to eat something but she didn't think she could be bothered.

She had just settled on the sofa with Poppy and a mug of hot chocolate when she heard the tell-tale signs of a vehicle driving into the yard.

With a sigh she put down her mug and climbed off the sofa. There was a gentle knock at the door and Ruth opened it. She plastered a smile on her face. This was what she was here for, to take in animals out of hours and to nurse them back to health. She wasn't going to let some person take that from her.

'How can I help?' she asked as she pulled the door open.

'Actually, I thought you might need cheering up,' Tom said, holding up a bottle of wine and a plastic bag, which by the smell of it contained an Indian takeaway.

Friends Reunited

Ruth just stared. If she had had to guess who was at her door, then Tom would have been one of her last guesses, after how things had ended last time they met.

'Look . . . I know that we both said some harsh things.'

Ruth raised an eyebrow. She was pretty sure all the harshness had come from him.

'OK, I said some things that now I've had chance to think about where not really what I meant. I saw the posters and the message,' he added as if that explained everything.

'And?' Ruth said.

'Your explanation seemed so far-fetched but now I'm starting to wonder if you were right.'

Ruth again raised an eyebrow. She wasn't in the mood to let him off easily.

'I think that someone is trying to ruin your reputation and I want to help.'

Ruth nodded and stood back so that

Tom could step inside. Poppy leapt to her feet as she caught sight of Colin who had been hiding in the shadows.

There was some barking and then the pair curled up in Poppy's basket besides the wood-burning stove.

'Colin was pining, too,' Tom said, placing the bag full of food on the small table. Ruth grabbed some plates and cutlery before finding two glasses.

'I really am sorry for what happened and I shouldn't have said what I did.'

'Thanks,' Ruth said and some of the worry eased at little. If Tom believed her, maybe others would. 'We really did find someone at the tip who sold our rubbish.'

'I know,' Tom said with some colour coming to his cheeks that Ruth was sure wasn't due to the wine. 'I went and asked myself.'

'Oh,' Ruth said. She couldn't exactly be annoyed that he had checked out the evidence but it did mean that he hadn't been prepared to take her word for it.

'And as soon as I did, I realised what

an idiot I had been.'

Ruth allowed herself a smile that was more like it.

'My only excuse is that Matilda is like my baby and I think I lost my head there for a bit.'

'Now that I can understand,' Ruth said as Tom poured red wine into each glass.

'So, friends?' Tom asked tentatively, raising his glass.

'Friends,' Ruth said and clinked her glass against his.

They ate the food, which was delicious, and talked about all sorts of things, and it was a relief to Ruth to be able to think about something other than her current situation, even for a little while.

'So what are you going to do?' Tom asked when they were sitting side by side on the sofa.

'I'm not sure there is anything I can do,' Ruth said with a sigh. 'Sam is going to see if she can identify who the message writer is.'

Tom nodded.

'Apparently one of her kids is a computer whizz.'

'Have you thought about going to the police?' Tom asked.

Ruth stared. She hadn't even considered that.

'And say what?'

'Well fly tipping is an offence, for a start, and I'm sure there must be some kind of law around this sort of behaviour. Harassment or something?'

'I'm not sure the local police are going to be that interested and even if they were, would they have the resources to investigate something online?'

'You won't know till you ask,' Tom said thoughtfully.

'But what if it is someone I know?' Ruth said, wondering if she should mention Joe's theory. 'I'm not sure I want to get them into that kind of trouble.'

'They don't seem bothered by what they are doing to you,' Tom pointed out.

'Joe thinks it's Jeremy.' Ruth blurted out the words before she could change her mind. It had been a lovely evening and she didn't want to ruin it but at the same time she felt like there was an elephant in the room.

'I know,' Tom said with a small smile. Ruth let out her held in breath.

'And?' Ruth asked.

'It's not him, Ruth,' Tom said. There was no anger in his voice, it was just as if he were stating a simple fact. 'But there's bad blood between them and I'm not surprised Joe feels that way after everything that happened.'

'If that's true then why are you so sure it's not Jeremy? You know that he isn't exactly our biggest fan.'

Tom nodded and took a sip of wine.

'Because Jeremy made a mistake all those years ago. He knows now that it wasn't Joe that stole stuff but he can't bring himself to admit it. He's angry with himself, not with you or the sanctuary.'

Ruth frowned. That didn't make sense.

'Seeing Joe is a reminder of that fact. Jeremy is a good man, admittedly under layers of gruffness. And every time he sees Joe or you, he is reminded that he made a terrible mistake.

'It broke my dad's heart and he has never been able to forgive himself.'

'He might feel better if he told Joe that,' Ruth said. 'I know Joe would feel better.'

'He's a proud man, as well. I can't see him doing that.' Now it was Tom's turn to sigh. 'But I'm working on him.'

'The thing is, Jeremy is the only person who has ever had anything negative to say about the sanctuary. If it's not him, then who is it?'

'That is what we need to find out,' Tom said.

Ruth's heart missed a beat at the term 'we'.

'I figure it's the least I can do.' Tom turned to look at Ruth and Ruth hoped that she was hiding how she felt. She nodded. 'And besides, I'm involved, too. Matilda was injured by this idiot. Who knows what he will do next? We need to stop him.'

'I agree,' Ruth said. 'The only problem is how we go about that.'

'Well, I took photos of the rubbish that was dumped before we cleared it. I thought we could go through them and see if there was anything that wasn't yours. There might be a clue as to the identity of the dumper.'

It was a long shot but it was worth a try.

'I have them on my computer at home. We'll need to enlarge them to check out the small details. Would you be able to pop in tomorrow?' Tom asked.

'Sure. What time?' Ruth asked.

'About eleven? I should have finished the morning rounds then.'

'Eleven works for me. And whilst I'm there, I'll change those bandages for you.'

Tom looked down at his hands. They were still bandaged but in a very haphazard way.

'I did them myself,' he said with a grin.

'I can tell,' Ruth said, grinning back. The day had seemed like a disaster but had definitely improved.

'I'll be heading off, then.'

130

Ruth got to her feet as well and walked the few short paces to the door with Tom.

'And don't worry, we'll get to the bottom of this.'

'I hope so,' Ruth said, feeling an edge of worry creep into her voice.

'I promise,' Tom said. For a moment Ruth thought he was going to lean in and kiss her but he seemed to think better of it and instead laid a hand gently on her arm. They stood as they were for a second and then he left, leaving Ruth to imagine what a kiss might have felt like.

When Ruth told Joe what Tom had suggested he didn't look very impressed.

'Now he wants to help,' he said with a snort. 'Might have been nice if he had decided whose side he was on earlier.'

'I agree but he might be right. There may be a clue in the rubbish, you never know.'

'Aye, lass. No news from Sam yet?' he asked.

Ruth shook her head. All Sam had said was her son was working on it but he had had to stop to go to school and she couldn't exactly complain about that.

Ruth worked through the morning list as quickly as she could. She wasn't sure if it was her imagination but Joe seemed to be dragging his heels and she wondered if he didn't want her to go and see Tom.

She could understand that Tom wasn't exactly Joe's favourite person but it was just possible that there would some evidence in the photographs that could help them out.

Whoever was behind all this had been quiet for a couple of days and rather than being reassured, Ruth just felt like she was braced for the next thing all the time. She wanted to know who was behind all this and get them to stop.

She popped back into the cottage and changed into a clean top and fresh pair of jeans before whistling for Poppy, who appeared with a wagging tail.

'I won't be long,' Ruth said to Joe as she walked towards the back of the yard and to the path that would take her to Tom's farmhouse. Joe grunted in response.

'I've left sandwiches and cold drinks in the fridge. Can you make sure everyone gets something to eat?' She stopped walking, determined to get more than a grunt from Joe.

'Aye, lass, you know I will.'

'Make sure you take a proper break, too,' she said as she headed off down the path.

Poppy ran ahead and ran back, all the while with a dopey expression on her face. Ruth's relationship with Tom might have had some serious downs but the same could not be said for Poppy and Colin.

Ruth and Poppy reached the large yard in front of Tom's farmhouse and Colin dashed out of the open front door to greet them. Ruth laughed as Colin and Poppy took it in turns to chase each other.

'Ruth, hi,' Tom said through the open kitchen window. 'Come on inside. I have the kettle on.'

Ruth moved through the house and

into the farmhouse kitchen. It really did look as she always imagined the heart of a farmhouse would look. Even though it was a mild day, the range was putting out heat and the metal kettle was whistling away. At one end of the long table was a plate piled high with biscuits and Tom was lifting mugs to make the tea.

'Tea or coffee?' he asked.

'Tea, please.' Ruth looked around but couldn't see any sign of his laptop, which she thought was a bit odd but then a house this size probably had a study, unlike her own two-roomed cottage, where the front room doubled for pretty much everything other than sleeping.

'Help yourself to biscuits,' Tom said, sitting down on the bench opposite with a smile. 'I made them myself.'

Ruth looked at the pile to the polished wooden work surface that bore evidence of empty biscuit packets.

'Well, I would have . . . but who has the time?' he said, as they both laughed. 'Now I fear I may have dragged you over here under false pretences.'

'Oh?' Ruth asked, wondering if that was why there was no sign of the computer.

'I had a look at the photographs last night and there wasn't anything there that can help I'm afraid but hopefully the chocolate biscuits might soften the blow.'

Was it Ruth's imagination or did he look slightly uncomfortable?

The problem was, she wasn't sure whether it was because he could have rung her to tell her this and therefore their coffee meet up wouldn't have been necessary or because there was something in the photographs that he didn't want her to see.

Her heart wanted her to believe it was the former but she had suspicions that it was the latter. She felt a little cross with Joe. She usually took people at their word but Joe seemed to think that anyone connected to McMillan's was up to something and now it seemed that she was starting to think that way, too.

'That's a shame. I was really hoping

there would be.'

'I hope you don't mind coming over. I was looking forward to us meeting up again.'

'I was, too,' Ruth said, glad that Poppy had trotted in at that moment and given her an excuse to look anywhere other than at Tom.

She was sure that she would see in his face whether he had similar feelings to her own or if perhaps he was just making excuses. Right now, she didn't want to know which it was.

Colin appeared, too, and trotted over to Tom, laying his furry head in Tom's lap. Tom scratched his ears and Ruth risked a glance in his direction. If there was any clue to be had from Tom's face it was gone now, replaced by a contented, soft smile.

'I like you, Ruth.' Tom's voice cut through the companionable silence and Ruth blinked in surprise.

'I like you, too,' Ruth said, her heart starting to beat out a funny sort of dance.

'I mean I . . . really like you,' Tom said

and now he looked up at her and she could see that he meant it.

Ruth nodded and smiled as no words would come in that moment. Tom reached across the table and Ruth slipped her hand into his.

'So maybe we could see some more of each other?' Tom asked tentatively.

'I'd like that,' Ruth said, 'but only after I fix your terrible attempts at bandaging.'

The bandages on Tom's hands weren't exactly clean and they looked as though they had been applied by a small child playing doctor with their teddy bear. Tom looked at them and laughed and to Ruth, it was the best sound she had ever heard.

All is Revealed?

Ruth walked home across the fields, feeling like everything was right in her world. She pulled at some long grasses as she passed and Poppy, with her nose to the ground, ran on ahead. The sun was out and the promise of a fresh start was in the air.

She glanced then at her watch and realised she had been rather longer than she had planned and quickened her pace.

She wasn't a doe-eyed teenager dealing with her first crush, who lost sight of everything else in her life. She needed to focus on the other important thing in her life, the wildlife sanctuary.

She walked into the yard and could see a car parked in front of the first shed. She jogged across to the shed that had become the reception area, a place where she could initially assess any animals that came in.

'What do we have?' she asked as she opened the door. Barbara and Joe looked up. An anxious woman carrying a small child on her hip tried to smile.

'I don't know if I did the right thing,' she said. 'I know that you are supposed to leave them, that their mums will usually come back for them but it was over twenty-four hours and I couldn't just leave him.'

Ruth gave a reassuring smile and walked to the metal table. On the top was a cardboard box and inside was an old jumper and a small brown fox cub. Joe had on some stiff gloves and gently lifted the cub from its protective cocoon.

'Eyes closed,' Joe said. 'No sign of the mother?' he asked the woman, his tone kind.

'We looked. There have been some foxes killed on the main road.'

'Chances are parents have been killed. You did the right thing bringing her in. Once they are a little older it's best to keep them in the wild and feed them with dog food but at this age they won't stand a chance in the wild,' Ruth said, checking the cub. There were no obvious injuries but despite the jumper she felt a little cold.

'Can you have a look around when you get home to check for more?' Joe said to the woman who nodded. 'There may be more in the litter. If you find them just give us a ring and I'll come and collect them, save you a journey.'

'Thank you,' the lady said with a smile. 'Would it be OK to check in and see how she is doing?'

'Of course,' Barbara said, 'and bring the children. They are never too young to learn about wildlife.'

'I'll take her on,' Joe said to Ruth. Ruth nodded.

It was important to keep fox cubs as wild as possible so they would have a dedicated volunteer so they didn't get too used to humans. She knew that Joe would keep the fox's long term future in mind and avoid treating her like a pet, however cute she was.

'Do you want to take her to the incubators? I'll make up the formula and bottle.'

140

Joe nodded as he carefully wrapped up the cub and carried her outside.

Once the cub was settled and Joe had named her Betty, Ruth put the kettle on.

'So how did it go with McMillan?' Joe asked. The newest arrival seemed to have mellowed him a little.

'No luck, I'm afraid,' Ruth said.

She had thought she might share her fears with Joe about not getting to see the photos herself but since Tom had made his feelings clear she didn't want anything to ruin how she felt.

And Joe was highly likely to suspect that Tom was hiding something. The problem for Ruth was that she wasn't 100 percent sure that he wasn't.

'Well, Sam will be in later tonight and maybe that boy of hers will have found something out.' Joe sipped his tea.

'And at least nothing else has happened,' Barbara pointed out as she gratefully accepted her own mug. 'And it doesn't seem to have stopped the locals bringing in wildlife.

'We've had some more birds come in

this morning and I think we will be getting some overflow from the main centre, too.'

Ruth nodded. This was the start of the busiest season of the year. The oldest youngsters would be getting ready for release all the while new babies would be arriving.

'How's the roster looking?' she asked.

'Pretty good. There are a few gaps where we might have to do double shifts but that's fine,' Barbara said with a smile and Ruth thought once more that she had no idea how she would cope without her small team of dedicated animal lovers.

Joe put down his tea cup and stood up.

'I need to head home for a couple of hours. Got the gas man coming. Will you be all right?'

'Of course,' Ruth said with a smile. 'Don't be late back for dinner, though.'

'As if I would, lass, as if I would.' Joe nodded to them both and walked away to his small van, which doubled as a wildlife ambulance at times.

'So I don't need to ask how it went with Tom since it is written all over your face,' Barbara said mildly before helping herself to a biscuit. Ruth frowned.

'Was it that obvious?'

'To a person with grown-up daughters, yes.' Barbara smiled. 'He's a good man, I like him.'

'I do, too.'

'But?' Barbara asked. Ruth looked at her. There was no judgement on Barbara's face, just interest and concern. 'Something's obviously bothering you.'

Ruth sighed.

'Well, you know I went over to look at the photographs?' Barbara nodded. 'Well, when I got there, he said he had already looked at them and there was nothing that could help.'

Barbara nodded again.

'So he just wanted an excuse to see you again?' Barbara asked with a small smile.

'I think so. It's just there is a very small part of me that wonders if there

143

was something there but he just didn't want me to see it.'

'Ah. What did he say?'

'He said he really liked me.'

'And I can see that you like him,' Barbara said, taking a sip of tea to try to hide her smile but failing.

'I do but what if that small part of me is right?' Ruth looked out over the yard, taking in each hard earned part of the sanctuary. Would she risk this place, which she loved and had sacrificed so much for, for Tom?

If he was hiding something, perhaps the attacks would keep coming? Maybe she would never get to the bottom of things, and in the long term that might do some serious damage to her dream here.

'Well, my opinion, for what it's worth, is that love is a risk and requires a certain amount of trust.'

Ruth groaned and looked at her feet.

'I've never been very good at that. It's like a part of me always expects to get hurt.'

'You don't have to go all in straight away, love. Right now it's about baby steps. Do you trust him enough to risk seeing him again?'

Ruth thought about this and then nodded. She wanted to see him again, to see what they might have together.

'Then, I would suggest, that is all you need to know right now.'

Ruth felt some of the tension leave her as Barbara's words sank in.

'Has anyone ever told you how wise you are?'

Barbara laughed.

'Wisdom comes when you have daughters and it's hard earned, too.'

'Thank you.'

Ruth held up her mug as if it were a glass of champagne and Barbara knocked her mug against it. They smiled and enjoyed a moment of peace and quiet before a car pulled into the yard and Sam jumped out.

Ruth waved as Sam jogged over.

'You're early for your shift,' Ruth said, glancing at her watch to check that she hadn't lost track of time so badly that it was in fact past six.

'I have news,' Sam said, waving some sheets of paper and sounding breathless. Ruth and Barbara exchanged glances.

'Please tell me that Mr Anonymous isn't up to his old tricks again?' Ruth said, shaking her head. It wouldn't surprise her if he was, he had after all been quiet for a few days.

'No — and he isn't Mr Anonymous any more.'

Ruth stared. She knew that one of Sam's boys was a whizz at all things computer related but she hadn't allowed herself to consider that he might actually be able to find out who was behind it all. She thought the inevitable disappointment might be too much.

'Sam, sit down and I'll make you a cup of tea. Get your breath back,' Barbara said, getting to her feet and gesturing that Sam should sit in her place, 'but don't say anything until I get back.'

Her voice carried from the inside of the cottage where Ruth could hear her

146

putting the kettle on.

Ruth wriggled in her seat, waiting for Barbara to come back. She was desperate to know what information Sam had but at the same time she was worried. If it turned out to be someone she knew, someone she liked or respected, she wasn't sure how she would cope.

Somehow it was easier to have a nameless, faceless enemy than to discover that someone you believed to be your friend was in fact the opposite.

Barbara handed over the steaming cup of tea and Sam took a grateful sip.

'Well, I don't understand any of the computer speak. Tim tried to explain it to me but it went way over my head,' Sam said.

'Who is it?'

'Each computer has a sort of address and Tim was able to work out who the address belongs to,' Sam said and Ruth had the feeling that she was stalling, that now she was here she didn't want to break the news. Ruth felt her stomach drop. It couldn't be Tom, could it? That would make no sense whatsoever.

'Please tell me it's not Tom,' she blurted out.

Sam gave her a look.

'It's not Tom, Ruth. It's Jeremy.'

For a moment all Ruth could hear was wind rushing in her ears as black dots danced in front of her eyes. Joe was right. She should have listened to him. Jeremy was behind it all.

After all, he was the only one who had ever been openly hostile about the idea of the sanctuary. He had history with Joe to and whatever Tom's explanations, Jeremy had driven Joe out from a job that he loved.

'You OK, love?' Barbara asked, her face a picture of concern.

'Yes,' Ruth managed to say faintly as she fought to pull herself together. 'It's not really that much of a surprise. Joe said all along it was him.'

'The question now is — what we are going to do about it?' Sam asked.

'We could go and speak to him, on the quiet. Perhaps once he knows that we know, he'll stop.'

'We should go to the police.' Joe's voice made them all jump as they hadn't seen him approach. 'What he's done is criminal and he should be dealt with as such.'

'I know you have history with him, Joe,' Barbara said, 'but surely it's better if we deal with this discreetly than make a big thing of it?'

Joe snorted.

'The next thing you'll suggest is that we let burglars off because they had a hard time at home. No, Barbara, what he's done is wrong and he needs to be punished.'

Ruth's thoughts were whirling around in her head.

'I need time to think about this,' she said softly and everyone looked at her. 'Even though Joe said it was Jeremy all along, it's still a bit of a shock,' she added by way of explanation.

Joe's expression softened a little.

'Aye, lass, you take your time but if you ask me you know what you need to do.'

'I'm going to go and start the dinner. If you are all OK?'

The three nodded without saying a word and Ruth escaped to the cottage, glad to be alone to try and work out what she was going to do next.

Anger and Mistrust

Even the next day, Ruth had no real idea what she was going to do. All night she had tried to think of reasons why Tom hadn't wanted to show her the photos and the only one that made any sense was that he had seen something that would connect the dumped rubbish with Jeremy.

It was clear that Tom and Jeremy shared a tight bond but still Ruth couldn't think why he hadn't told her. He had been quick enough to accuse her of dumping the rubbish but he seemed reluctant to do the same with Jeremy, even when there was clear evidence he was at fault.

Of course, Tom had only known Ruth for a few weeks and he had grown up beside Jeremy so maybe it wasn't a surprise where his loyalty lay. None of this stopped Ruth feeling hurt and betrayed, though. If Tom had told her, she was sure they could have worked something out.

Ruth had made it clear that she didn't want the person punished, just wanted them to stop. It seemed that Tom didn't trust her and that hurt more than anything. Ruth sighed. She knew that Joe and the others would expect her to have come up with an answer by now but if anything she was more confused than ever.

'You look like you didn't get much sleep,' Sam said as Ruth brought out the morning coffee for the volunteers.

'I'm fine — just trying to work out what we should do.'

'No rush, Ruth. It looks like he's gone quiet so you have time to decide, whatever Joe might think.'

Joe was currently in with the young badgers and so was out of earshot.

'What do you think I should do?' she asked Sam, knowing that she might not have another chance later with other people around.

'Well, we need it to stop, right?'

Ruth nodded.

'But I'm guessing you don't fancy involving the police?'

Ruth shrugged. She wasn't sure what she thought any more, except for a deep desire for it to be over and dealt with.

'So the way I see it you have a choice. You speak to Tom and let him deal with it. Jeremy is his employee, after all.'

Ruth tried not to let her emotions at the thought of that show on her face but when Sam smiled kindly at her, she knew she had failed.

'Or you confront Jeremy directly.'

Ruth pulled a grimace.

'I'm not sure which is worse.'

'Well, one of us could deal with it for you. I wouldn't mind having a word.'

Ruth shook her head.

'That's a really sweet offer but I should do it. You already do more than I could ever expect, there is no way I'm going to ask you to do something I'm too chicken to do.'

Sam reached out and laid her hand on Ruth's arm.

'Ruth, you are one of the bravest

people I have ever known. You can do this but do it in your own time and in your own way. Don't let anyone bully you into anything different,' Sam said, throwing a glance in Joe's direction as he came out of the badger shed.

'Joe loves you but when it comes to Jeremy all his good sense goes out of the window.'

Ruth nodded and smiled. She was so grateful for not just the help the volunteers provided but for the feeling of family they created, too, something she had been missing since she lost her dad.

'Morning, lass,' Joe said, walking over. 'I think you might need to take a look at the dressing on the little one. Looks like he might have been having a nibble at it and we don't want him to get it off.'

'I'll take a look. I need to review all the hedgehogs today as well. They all need weighed.'

Sam smiled at this. Ruth knew the hedgehogs were her favourite and that Sam was already eyeing up who she was going to re-home in her back garden.

'I expect Sam will want to help you with that,' Joe said and they all laughed.

There was the sound of wheels on gravel and Tom's battered old Range Rover came into view. The three of them turned to stare at it.

Ruth tried to remember if they had set any dates or time for their next meet up but she didn't think they had. Tom climbed out of the car with a wide grin, which dropped a little when he saw the look on everyone's faces.

Joe butted in.

'You've got a right cheek turning up here!' he said, his voice loud and his anger obvious. 'Did you think we were too stupid to work it out? Did you think you could pull the wool over Ruthie's eyes?'

Tom was walking towards them looking around and obviously aware that some of the other volunteers had moved so that they could both see and hear what was going on.

'Perhaps we could discuss this in private?' Tom directed the comment to

Ruth. The problem was in that moment Ruth was seeing red.

All the hurt was quickly turning into anger. He had lied to her, tried to cover it up and then tried to distract her from the fact by claiming to have feelings for her. The small amount of doubt she had had at the time was now beginning to grow.

'Since it affects everyone here perhaps you should just tell us all the truth?' Ruth said, her anger that had burned so hot had dampened a little when she saw the hurt on Tom's face.

'I really can explain . . .' Tom started to say.

'I bet,' Joe said sarcastically.

'Joe,' Ruth said a warning tone, 'let Tom speak.' In that moment she couldn't think of a reasonable explanation for his actions but there was still a part of her that was desperate to hear that there was one.

'How much do you know?' Tom asked and Ruth blinked. She wasn't expecting him to ask that.

Joe snorted.

'Why do you want to know?' He shook his head. 'You're just stalling for time to come up with some story. We know it all, mate, and I can't see you or your friend wriggling out of this one.'

The yard suddenly became very silent as if no-one quite knew what to say next. Tom looked at Ruth and she felt caught in his gaze. She wanted to believe him, that there was a reason, a very good reason, for why he had tried to keep the truth from her. She needed him to say something.

'Sounds like you have already made up your mind,' Tom said.

'You haven't really said anything that would make me see it differently,' Ruth pointed out.

'You haven't given me much of a chance.'

Ruth spread her arms wide as if to say 'Now is your chance' but Tom shook his head.

'I thought that we were friends. That you would at least give me the benefit of the doubt.'

'Like you did, when the rubbish was dumped on your land?' Ruth spat the words out and instantly regretted them.

They might be true but it wasn't going to help the situation. The problem was the anger and the hurt were making it hard to think straight. Joe's take on it seemed to make sense and it wasn't as if Tom was saying anything to change her mind.

Tom and Ruth glared at each other for a few seconds, both too angry to be the one to make the first move to an apology.

'Fine,' Tom said. 'I can see it's not worth my time trying to convince you since you are sure you are right.'

He threw a look at Joe which was a mixture of fury and pain and then marched back to his car. He slammed the door and drove out of the yard just a little too fast.

'Good riddance!' Joe shouted after the car but Ruth could see that Tom's expression had shaken the man a little.

Ruth felt like a deflated balloon. All

the anger had fizzled out and left behind hurt and confusion. Worse, she knew she had behaved like a child and not really given Tom a chance to explain.

The way that things were, she didn't imagine that she would have the opportunity to ask him why he had lied to her.

'Why don't I make us all a cuppa? I think we need something after that,' Sam said, giving Ruth's arm a quick squeeze.

'You go ahead. I'm going to walk the paddock to check the fence in case we get any larger animals in,' Ruth said, walking away before anyone could see her tears.

A Tense Rescue

The good news was that there had been no activity from 'Mr Anonymous' since Ruth had last seen Tom. The bad news was that she felt like her heart had been broken in two.

She knew she was being daft. Her relationship with Tom had taken just a tentative step on from being friends but to her it felt like a decades-old romance had come to an end. Ruth was sure that in part it was due to the way it had ended. She had seen glimpses of Tom driving his car down the lane but she hadn't acknowledged that she had seen him and Tom had ignored her, too.

Even Joe had been quiet and Ruth tried to put a brave face on things when he was around. Joe had every right to react like he had after all he had been through at the hands of Jeremy and he didn't need to feel guilty that Ruth was now heartbroken.

Not that it was his fault at all but Ruth

knew Joe well enough to understand that he would take that burden on. So this morning Ruth was determined to be more upbeat.

'Morning, Joe, how are the hoglets today?' she asked as she stepped out of the front door of the cottage.

'Putting on weight nicely. It's probably time to separate some of the older ones and get them ready for their release.'

'Excellent. I had a phone call late last night to say that a family had found some abandoned babies and they were going to bring them in this morning.'

''Tis the season,' Joe said with a smile. 'And they'll keep coming for a while. How you doing, lass?' Joe asked after a moment of silence.

'Much better, thanks,' Ruth said with a smile and for the first time in a few days she felt less like she was acting the role of someone who was fine.

'I've been thinking about it and I may have spoken out of turn.'

'Joe, you have every right to be angry with Jeremy. What he did then was awful and then what he has done since.' Ruth shook her head at the thought.

'Aye, but I didn't need to take it out on Tom. He's always been in the middle and he's a loyal man. Jeremy may be a lot of things but he was good to that boy.'

'Let's give it some time. I'm sure we can work things out with Tom.' Ruth wasn't sure but she did hope and that was almost the same thing, wasn't it?

'I hope so, lass. I hate to be the cause of heartache.'

Ruth stood in front of Joe and made him look her in the eye.

'Any heartache is down to me and Tom, Joe. Nothing to do with you or anything you said. In truth we both behaved liked teenagers, not giving each other the chance to speak, not prepared to listen. So I don't want you worrying about that, OK?'

Ruth waited until Joe finally nodded his head before stepping out of his way.

'Right, let's go get ready for our next set of guests, shall we?'

Joe grinned at the thought and Ruth

could only hope that he had taken her words to heart.

★ ★ ★

The day had been so busy with new arrivals that Ruth and Joe had barely had enough time to stop and eat their lunch.

'Right, you two. Sit down right now and drink your tea,' Barbara ordered and Joe and Ruth didn't need telling twice. They both slumped down on the bench outside the cottage to catch their breath.

'Anyone who said this place wasn't needed should have been here today,' Joe said with a wry smile.

'It's a good job some of our guests are nearly ready to move on — we are almost at capacity,' Ruth said, stretching out her legs in front of her.

Barbara appeared with a tray of tea and some home-made cake.

'Where's Poppy?' Barbara asked.

'Asleep by the wood-burner I expect,' Ruth said, smiling at the thought of her dog who had the ability to sleep for many hours of the day.

'She's not there,' Barbara said, 'and I peeked into your bedroom as well.'

Ruth put her cup of tea down and stood up.

'Poppy?' she called and waited for the bark which would tell her that Poppy had heard her and was on her way but there was nothing. The skin on Ruth's arms prickled. She called Poppy's name again but there was nothing. She turned and looked at Joe and could see concern on his face.

'Don't worry, lass, she'll be around here somewhere. She might even have managed to get shut in one of the sheds. You know how she likes to sneak in when you aren't looking.'

Half an hour later and Ruth was trying not to let her panic show but she knew she was failing. Poppy never ran away and she always stayed in earshot.

'Perhaps I should check out on the lane, maybe with the cars . . .' Ruth couldn't bear to finish her sentence.

'No need, I've already done it and

there's no sign of her. Besides, she's got more sense than that,' Joe said gruffly.

All of the volunteers had now stopped work and searched everywhere they could think of but there was no sign of Poppy.

'Perhaps she's gone out over the fields?' Barbara asked. 'She does have a bit of a thing for Tom's dog — maybe she's gone looking for him.'

Ruth had been dreading seeing Tom again. She had no idea what she would say or how awkward it might be but if she saw Tom now with Poppy at his side she thought she would simply run up and kiss him.

'I'll head that way and see if I can see her.'

'I'll go over the woods. Take your phone and let us know if you find her,' Joe said.

'Call me here,' Barbara said, 'and I'll coordinate.'

They all nodded and headed off in their assigned directions. Ruth was call-ing Poppy's name and getting more and more desperate. She was becoming convinced that something terrible had happened to her beloved pet.

She heard Tom before she saw him.

'Colin!' and then a whistle.

Ruth hurried in the direction of the sound.

'Tom? Have you seen Poppy?' Ruth said as he came into view. In that moment any concern of meeting him again was gone.

'No — and Colin has mysteriously disappeared, too. Totally unlike him.'

Tom's concern echoed her own.

'I almost feel a little better if I know they are together.'

Tom nodded.

'I've got the guys out looking and I said I'd walk the boundary. Since it seems they are together do you want to come with me?' His words were tentative as if he had the same feeling she did about their first meeting, as if he wasn't sure how it would turn out either.

Ruth nodded and fell into step. Between them, they took it in turns to call out their dog's name.

They walked on for at least a mile and there was no sign of their dogs.

'I'm sorry,' Tom said out of the blue. Ruth looked up at him.

'Me, too,' Ruth said. 'I know I behaved like a teenager.'

'Me, too,' Tom said.

'Let's find them then maybe we can talk about it.'

'Good plan,' Tom said.

'Poppy!' Ruth yelled and Tom grabbed her arm.

'Did you hear that?'

They both froze and strained their ears to listen. Ruth was about to speak and then she heard it too.

'Poppy?' she tried again. And then she was sure she heard it. She broke into a run and Tom easily kept up beside her.

'I think it's Colin,' he said. Colin continued to bark in reply and they were able to pinpoint where he was.

Colin was running towards them and then running back the way he had come.

'It must be Poppy,' Tom said and

speeded ahead. Ruth saw Tom drop to his knees and she was at his side in seconds. Colin licked her face once and then turned his attention back to Poppy.

Tom and Ruth were kneeling by a deep hole in the ground. It was too square to be natural and around eight feet deep. Poppy was at the bottom and judging by the scrambling marks on the earth walls, had been trying to climb out for some time. At the sight of Ruth's face she started to whine and pace.

'Oh, sweetheart! How on earth did you get down there?' Poppy whimpered and pawed at the sides. 'Don't worry, we'll get you out,' Ruth said confidently and then looked at Tom.

She didn't know how but she would get her out. It was too deep for one of them to climb down. If they did they would likely get stuck down there too.

'Here,' Tom said, handing Ruth a bottle of water. 'She must be thirsty by now. See if you can get some water down to her. I'm going to run back to the farm and get some kit so we can get her out.'

Ruth took the water bottle and nodded.

'I'll be as quick as I can.'

Ruth flashed him a quick grateful smile and then tried to figure out how to get water down to Poppy. She heard Tom's footsteps run and felt a small warm body join her at the edge of the pit.

'Hey, Colin, you're a good friend you know. Finding Poppy and leading us to her.'

Colin licked her nose and then lay flat, paws just over the edge and stared down at Poppy. Ruth looked around the woodland and spotted something in the undergrowth.

Seeing litter normally made her feel so cross but today she felt relieved. It was a plastic one pint milk bottle. She grabbed it and then pulled her pocket knife from her pocket, cutting off the top but leaving the handle whole.

She had to wander further afield looking for something she could use to lower it down but eventually found a branch which had a sort of hooked small branch that would do.

Carefully she filled the milk bottle and gently lowered it down. For a moment Poppy sniffed at it suspiciously but then started to take small delicate slurps. Ruth poured the rest of the water into her cupped hand and let Colin drink. She had no idea how long he had been out here, either.

'It's OK, Pops,' she said, 'Tom is coming back and he is going to help me get you out.' Just saying the words out loud made her feel tearful. It was a mixture of relief that Poppy was all right, albeit stuck down a hole, and the sense that she might not have found her without Colin and Tom's help.

There was a sound of someone crashing through the undergrowth and Tom appeared, flushed and slightly breathless.

'I've asked some of my guys to come out here and sort out the hole. We don't want any wildlife falling down into it.'

Tom had to two lengths of strong rope over his shoulder and what looked like

170

his washing basket. Ruth watched as he tied a rope to each side of it.

'It was the best I could come up with at short notice and I didn't want to leave Poppy down there any longer. The guys are going to bring over some more kit, in case this doesn't work.'

Ruth nodded as Tom handed her one of the ropes and held on to the other himself.

'We just need to get her to climb in,' Tom said as between them they lowered the basket into the pit.

Initially Poppy backed away from the strange object that was being lowered down but with some encouragement from Ruth she came over and started to sniff it.

'Come on, Poppy, we need you to climb in, darling. Then we can raise you up.'

Poppy walked around the edge but showed no signs of wanting to climb in.

'Poppy, please,' Ruth said, feeling the tears coming back. Colin was barking his encouragement but Poppy still didn't seem to trust the basket. Tom looked at Colin.

'I have an idea. Let's pull it back up.'

Ruth couldn't see what the plan was but pulled her side so that the basket was back up with them. Without being told, Colin climbed in the basket and barked. Tom scratched him behind the ears.

'Good boy. We'll lower you down. Then you get out and get Poppy to climb in. We'll pull Poppy up and then send the basket back down for you.'

Colin barked once and Ruth couldn't help a little smile. It seemed that Tom also spoke to his dog as if he understood every word.

Between them they manoeuvred the basket over the edge. It wobbled a lot and Ruth was surprised that Colin didn't try to jump out but they managed to lower him to the floor of the pit.

Colin jumped out and he and Poppy had an enthusiastic reunion which involved running around the small space and barking. Then Colin started to shepherd Poppy towards the basket. Poppy

172

was still reluctant but Colin kept pushing and nudging her and eventually she climbed in.

'Right,' Tom said, 'nice and gently now.'

They pulled together and slowly the basket moved up the side of the hole and then it was at the top. Ruth gathered Poppy in her arms and buried her face in her fur.

'Is she OK?' Tom asked.

Ruth ran her hands all over her dog, checking for injuries.

'She seems to be.'

'Let's get Colin,' Tom said and they both looked down to see Colin sitting in the basket, patiently waiting his turn. They hauled him up and he threw himself first at Tom and then at Poppy.

Tom and Ruth both laughed as the dogs ran around in circles but staying carefully away from the pit edge.

'I'm so glad she's OK.'

'I wouldn't have found her without your help,' Ruth said and it was as if all her defences collapsed at once and she found herself unable to hold back the sob.

Tom drew her into his arms and held her, his chin resting on the top of her head. Ruth didn't think she had felt so safe for a long time and wasn't sure she could ever bear to let go but then the two dogs were nudging in between them.

'I think they're looking for a group hug,' Tom said and so they both knelt down and did a two-person, two-dog hug.

'Colin, you are a very good dog and a very good friend,' Ruth said seriously.

'And I think we are both sorry that we have kept the pair of you apart,' Tom said and he looked to Ruth who nodded.

'It's my fault,' Ruth said. 'I should have given you a chance to speak.'

'I shouldn't have hidden the photos from you. That's not what friends do,' Tom said.

Ruth wanted to ask why he had but a couple of guys who worked for Tom appeared and she didn't think it was the kind of conversation that either of them wanted to have with an audience.

'Deer pit,' the older guy said, taking a look.

'That's what I thought,' Tom said, 'but they were all covered up years ago.'

'Aye, we made wooden covers for 'em. Maybe someone decided to help themselves to the wood?' the older guy said.

'I'd like it properly filled, I think. I know my dad thought that we should keep them in case the deer became a problem but it's not the way I want to farm. And besides that, they didn't work and caused suffering to other animals.'

The two guys nodded. They had brought wheelbarrows and shovels with them.

'If you can mark out the rest of the pits, I'll come out tomorrow and work on filling the rest.'

'I'll help,' Ruth said, 'and I'm sure Joe will want to lend a hand.'

'That would be great, thanks. In the meantime, why don't we head back to the farmhouse? I think we could all do with a drink and something to eat.'

Hatching a Plan

As they walked back through the woods, Tom reached out for Ruth's hand and she made no objections. It seemed a kind of perfect way to travel, walking along with two dogs and someone you thought you might love. Neither of them spoke but it was a comfortable silence. They knew they had lots to talk about but the walk was too perfect to interrupt.

It was only when the farmhouse appeared before them that she realised she hadn't phoned Joe or anyone at the sanctuary to tell them she had found Poppy.

'I need to phone . . .' Ruth said, letting go of Tom's hand and reaching for her mobile.

'Relax, I called when I came back for the stuff. Spoke to Barbara and she was going to ring Joe.'

Ruth looked at Tom, so glad that he had been so thoughtful when she had been too wrapped up in the moment to think about her friends who were worried and searching.

'Thank you,' Ruth said, 'for everything.'

'That's what friends do,' Tom said with a warm smile. His eyes danced as if he too felt there was more between them than just friendship.

Tom opened the door and set about making the tea. Ruth filled up the water bowl and the dogs took it in turns to drink loudly.

'There are treats in the tin. I think they both deserve some,' Tom said.

Both dogs sat to attention and were well rewarded for their bravery. When it seemed that the treat supply had run out they curled up in the one basket together and seemed to be asleep in moments.

'Too much excitement for one day,' Tom said, placing two mugs on the long kitchen table. Ruth took the seat opposite and helped herself to a biscuit from the plate that Tom had put out.

'The thing I don't get is that Poppy has never run off like that before,' Ruth said, glancing at the basket, needing to remind herself that Poppy was safe.

'Neither has Colin. I hate to say it but I think our dogs are in love.'

Ruth laughed.

'I think you're right. To avoid any more drama maybe we should make sure that they get to see each other every day.'

'I'd like that,' Tom said with shining eyes.

'So would I,' Ruth said, feeling a little shy all of a sudden.

'I need to explain about the photos,' Tom said, looking at Ruth.

'I know you must have had a good reason it's just in the moment I couldn't see it.'

'I did but I still should have told you.' Tom sighed and took a sip of tea. 'I'm guessing you have figured out where the messages posted to the website were coming from.'

Ruth nodded slowly.

'Jeremy posted them.'

'I know that it looks that way — but it wasn't him.'

178

'Are you saying that someone is trying to frame Jeremy for all this?' Ruth couldn't keep the incredulity from her voice. This was not a blockbuster movie, with twists and turns.

If the messages had been traced back to Jeremy's house then it had to be him. Surely no-one locally had the skills to make it look like the messages came from Jeremy's house.

'Yes, I am,' Tom said.

Ruth was waiting for him to laugh and say that it was all a joke. She wasn't sure that they were quite ready to joke about the situation but she could forgive him that. But if he was about to spin her another lie in the shape of a story she wasn't sure she could cope with that.

'OK,' Ruth said, making herself speak slowly, 'and why would someone want to do that? Assuming that it is even possible.'

'Jeremy is not without enemies.'

Ruth took a deep breath and counted to ten in her head. She didn't want to fall out with Tom again and had promised she would listen to him but what he was saying just seemed downright out-rageous.

'I guess we can agree that he doesn't always go out of his way to make friends with people, but enemies? Really?'

'I wouldn't say that you were the sort of person who had enemies but someone has been targeting you,' Tom pointed out and in some respects it was a reasonable point.

But Ruth still wasn't sure she could buy into the idea that there was a much more complicated, nefarious plan behind it all.

Ruth sighed. After everything that had happened she didn't want to reach the same impasse again but she just wasn't sure she could believe that someone was going to such extreme lengths to frame Jeremy.

Especially since the only people who seemed negatively affected were Tom, Ruth and the sanctuary.

'But it doesn't seem to be affecting Jeremy all that much,' Ruth pointed out, determined to stay reasonable. Poppy climbed out of the basket and dropped her head into Ruth's lap. Ruth wondered if she had detected the obvious tension between her and Tom again.

'So what do we do now?' Ruth asked, hoping that Tom would have some kind of answer to the problem.

'Make sure they get to see each other every day? Otherwise I have a feeling we will be chasing around after them a lot and I'm not sure that either of us have the time for that. Not to mention the fact that they seemed to get into mischief.'

'I agree, but that's not what I meant,' Ruth said, giving Tom a small smile to acknowledge that she knew he was trying to avoid the subject. Tom ran a hand through his hair and sighed.

'I know I have no right to ask you to do this but I was hoping you might be able to trust me — just for a couple of days to see if I can get to the bottom of what's going on.'

He looked her in the eyes and Ruth could feel her heart start to skip around in her chest. When he looked at her like that she knew she would agree to almost anything — but she also knew she needed to consider the work of the sanctuary.

It relied on the generosity and help of the locals, if that was lost due to Jeremy then it might not be possible to get it back and she didn't think she could give up on the dream she had shared with her dad.

Tom was looking at her and waiting patiently for an answer. There was no pressure in his expression and she thought he would accept whatever she decided, even if that was taking the evidence she had to the police.

'I'll hold off on any action on one condition . . .'

Ruth saw hope flare in Tom's eyes and she suspected it wasn't all about Jeremy. Could their fledgling attempt at a relationship survive if she reported his mentor to the police? She doubted it and that was one of the reasons she had agreed to give him more time.

'Anything,' Tom said and he looked

like he meant it.

'I want to be involved in the investigation.'

'Done,' Tom agreed and stretched his hand across the table. Ruth took it and shook it before they both laughed at their own silliness.

'OK, so where do we start?' Ruth asked.

'We start by talking to Jeremy,' Tom said with the look of a man about to go to the dentist for root canal work. Ruth knew the feeling. This was not going to be an easy conversation.

'Do you think he'll be happy to talk in front of me?' Ruth asked, not yet ready to let Tom tackle this by himself.

'No — but he doesn't have much choice now. It's too serious and he needs to know that if he doesn't help us figure out what is going on, then I will be reporting him to the police myself.'

Ruth blinked, not sure she had heard him correctly.

'He's my mentor, friend and has been like a father to me since I lost my dad but if he really did this then I don't know him at all.'

Tom's voice wavered a little on the last comment and all Ruth wanted to do was to hug him and take away the pain but Tom had stood up and she thought that maybe he was trying to hold it together and a hug wouldn't help.

'Then we need to get to the bottom of this, for all our sakes,' Ruth said as Tom led the way out of the farmhouse.

Surprising Confession

Tom climbed into the battered old Range Rover and Ruth got in the passenger side.

'Do you know where to find him?' Ruth asked.

'He's at home. He always pops home to see the kids after school,' Tom said.

Ruth couldn't hide the surprise on her face. She couldn't quite imagine that Jeremy had a family. He didn't seem to be the kind of person. Tom laughed at the look on her face.

'He's a devoted grandfather. His daughter moved in after she split up with her husband.'

'I wouldn't want to have been his son-in-law,' Ruth said.

'Let's just say that he told him exactly what he thought of him, even though by all accounts it was a joint decision between him and Maggie.'

'I have a feeling when it's your daughter and grandchildren, it doesn't really matter.'

'Exactly, although I think in truth he has been much happier since having the kids and Maggie around. It's one of the reasons we built the house for him.'

Ruth was struggling to imagine Jeremy even less happy than he was now, or perhaps she had only ever seen the worst of him?

They drove down one of the main farm tracks and then took a turning on the right through a small woodland. The woodland then opened up to a clearing and this was where Jeremy lived.

It was a modest farmhouse but the play equipment outside suggested that children lived there, too. There was a slide and a swing which hung from one of the large oak trees. All in all, Ruth thought it looked like a happy place.

As Tom pulled the car to a stop, two small children appeared from around the side of the house.

'Uncle Tom!' was the scream as the boy and the girl, who looked to be about eight, threw themselves in Tom's arms.

Tom must be used to it, Ruth thought, as he managed to grab them both and throw them in the air.

'Mummy didn't tell us you were coming,' the girl said as if that was a major black mark against her mum.

'Mummy didn't know,' Tom said.

'Where's Colin?' the boy asked.

'He's at home. He's been a bit naughty today so I left him there,' Tom said seriously. In truth Poppy and Colin had been fast asleep after their adventures and had showed no inclination to get out of their bed.

'Who's that?' the girl said, pointing at Ruth.

'This is my friend, Ruth,' Tom said, flashing Ruth a quick smile.

'Hello,' the girl said, suddenly coming over all shy. The boy held out his hand and Ruth shook it solemnly.

'Nice to meet you,' she said, trying to keep the smile from her face.

'Is Grandpa in?' Tom asked.

'Have you come to talk work?' the girl said, rolling her eyes at her brother.

187

'I'm afraid so,' Tom said, 'but I'll see you at the weekend.'

The children both nodded and then ran back around the house, obviously going back to whatever they were doing before.

'That's Tessa and Jacob. They're twins. Their brother Rob is the eldest, he's eleven and I expect he'll be up in his room playing computer games,' Tom said this as if he had no understanding of the concept. Ruth grinned. 'I know I'm out of touch, I just don't get it, when you've got all of this around you.'

'Yes, but you know eleven is practically a teenager these days and so it's probably what they're all doing.'

'So Maggie keeps telling me,' Jeremy said gruffly, appearing beside them. It was the first time he had ever even come close to agreeing with Ruth and she was so startled that she didn't know what to say.

'What brings you both out here?' Jeremy asked. His tone wasn't exactly friendly but it was probably the nicest

Jeremy had ever used around her.

'We need to talk to you about something.'

'Aye, I thought as much. Probably best not to speak of it here.' Jeremy gestured towards the house.

'Why don't we take a walk?' Tom suggested and Jeremy nodded.

They walked into the woods for about 10 minutes and nobody spoke. Ruth couldn't blame Tom. Now they were here, she didn't know how to start the conversation either, and it wasn't as if Jeremy were her close friend and mentor.

'I take it, it's about what's been happening around here,' Jeremy said. He had found a fallen log and taken a seat.

Ruth and Tom found similar spots and exchanged glances. At least he wasn't accusing Ruth of being the person who dumped the rubbish that had caused Matilda's injuries.

'It is,' Tom said slowly. 'Look, the thing is, Jeremy, there seems to be some evidence that points in your direction.'

Ruth had braced herself for an out-pouring of anger, and certainly if it wasn't him, she would have expected it. She had felt the same when she had been falsely accused.

'And what sort of evidence would that be?' Jeremy asked, looking at Tom and ignoring Ruth as if she wasn't there.

'There have been messages on the village website and they have been traced back to your computer.'

Jeremy didn't look particularly surprised or shocked, he just nodded.

'And?' Jeremy asked.

'And I was looking at the photos we took of the rubbish and well, let's just say, that seems to be a link to you, too.'

Jeremy nodded and Tom looked confused. Whatever he was expecting from Jeremy, it wasn't this.

'Tom doesn't believe it's you,' Ruth blurted out. She hated to see Tom struggle so much and Jeremy wasn't saying anything to defend himself.

'Then I'm sorry to disappoint you, lad, but it was me.' Jeremy was looking at the ground now and any fight there might have been had left him.

'I don't believe you,' Tom said.

'I thought you might say that but it doesn't make it any less true,' Jeremy said and now he looked up.

'And I owe you an apology, miss. I don't know what came over me but that's no excuse. I'm not a fan of some of what you do, rescuing things that cause farmers trouble but I had no right to do what I did and so for that I apologise.'

'Jeremy, this is serious . . .' Tom started to say.

'I know and I understand, miss, if you feel the need to involve the police. But whatever you decide I promise you there won't be any more trouble.'

With a nod, Jeremy was on his feet and was gone, striding off through the woods. Ruth watched him go and thought she could detect some relief in his stance. Perhaps relief that it was out in the open?

She shook her head. It didn't make sense; none of it made sense. Ruth turned to Tom, who was staring at nothing. His face was blank now as if he had no thoughts whatsoever.

'There's something more to this,' Ruth said after a few moments when it became clear that Tom was going to move or say anything.

'He just told you, Ruth. It was him. He did this.'

'I really don't think he did . . .' Ruth started to say but Tom was on his feet and his anger was obvious.

'For a little while, I actually believed him when he said that the rubbish dump was something to do with you.

'He let me believe him while all the while he knew the truth. He's made me look like a complete fool. The things I said . . .' Now Tom stopped talking and turned away, running a hand through his hair before clenching his fists.

'He's been like a father to me since my dad died. I just can't believe he would do this.'

'That's the point I'm trying to make, Tom, I don't think he did.'

Tom turned to face her and beneath the anger and hurt there was a flicker of hope.

'He and I may not see eye to eye on a lot of things but this, I don't think so.'

'That's not what you said before. That's not what Joe thinks.'

'We both know that Joe has every reason to feel the way he does but because of that it doesn't make his opinion the most balanced.'

Tom stared at her for a heartbeat and then nodded, somewhat reluctantly.

'But it's what you thought. too.'

'Well, I was influenced by Joe and to be honest, Jeremy was the only person who has ever been openly hostile to me about the sanctuary.'

Tom's shoulders dropped and he stared at the ground.

'Exactly. He is the only person it could be and not to mention the fact that he just admitted it.'

Tom kicked at a pile of leaves.

'But to me that doesn't seem to match with what just happened.'

Tom frowned.

'What just happened was he admitted it.

'Exactly,' Ruth said, willing Tom to look her in the eye and see what she was feeling. She didn't believe it was Jeremy and she couldn't bear to see Tom so hurt.

'You mean if he had done it, he wouldn't have admitted it?' Tom asked and he looked unconvinced.

'I don't think he would have been so contrite, somehow. I can't explain it. You know him better than me but this just doesn't feel right.'

Tom turned away again and started to pace up and down.

'He's a proud man but I would say he would admit it if he got it wrong.'

'OK. I may be reinforcing a stereotype but Jeremy doesn't seem to be the kind of man who is handy with a computer.'

Tom looked up sharply and there was the flicker of hope again. All Ruth could do now was pray that she was right about this. She wanted to be right so desperately, to protect Tom from the pain of being let down by a man he looked up to.

'He's a troglodyte,' Tom said, his eyes sparkling just a little.

'I thought so,' Ruth said, letting a small smile show on her face. 'In which case I doubt very much he would know how to post a comment on the village website.'

Tom nodded and then a thought seemed to strike down some of the burgeoning hope.

'But if it wasn't him, who was it?' Tom asked.

'There is a more important question you are overlooking,' Ruth said. Tom's face was a question mark but he said nothing. 'If it wasn't him, why has he taken the blame?'

Prime Suspect

They walked back to the farmhouse, considering all the possibilities.

'So it has to be someone that Jeremy knows, or why else would he take the blame?' Tom said as the farmhouse came into view.

'Who would he want to protect? A member of staff? Maybe after what happened with Joe all those years ago?'

Tom nodded and Ruth felt him reach down for her hand. She slipped her hand into his, marvelling at how it fitted, as if they had almost meant to be together.

'Perhaps. I know he carries the guilt around about Joe.'

'It's a shame he can't tell Joe, then maybe they could both put it behind them.'

'Two stubborn old men? Good luck with that.'

But Ruth knew she was going to have to try. If she and Tom were going to have a future together, then their two father figures were going to have to work out how to be in the same room without glaring at each other.

That was a problem for another day. Right now, they needed to work out why Jeremy was covering for someone else.

'So have any of your staff been acting oddly?' Ruth asked quietly as they crossed the farmyard. Tom lifted his hand up to a couple of guys who were manoeuvring the tractor.

'Not that I can tell. Most of them have been with me for years and the younger ones were all recommended by people. I would trust all of them.'

They stepped into the farmhouse and had to stop talking to give Colin and Poppy the fussing they demanded.

'It's hard, I know, but maybe give it some thought?'

Ruth glanced at her watch. She didn't want to go but she knew she really should. She had left the sanctuary in a panic about Poppy and even though Tom had phoned them she felt she ought to get back.

'I need to head back. I've been gone ages.'

'I'll walk you back,' Tom said and whistled Colin to his side. 'The dogs probably want to spend as much together as possible.'

Tom's smile gave the game away. It wasn't just the dogs that wanted to spend as much time together as possible. Tom reached for her hand and Ruth squeezed it to let him know that she felt the same.

As they walked around the fields in the sunshine, Ruth could almost forget everything else that was going on. If Jeremy was taking the blame for someone then she was sure that the anonymous attacks on the sanctuary would stop.

There would be no more posts accusing her of wrong-doing and no more rubbish dumps or posters. For that she felt relieved but she knew it wouldn't be completely over until they had worked out exactly what was going on, especially not for Tom.

'What are you going to tell the others?' Tom asked. They had been walking for some time, just enjoying each other's company and laughing at the dogs as they dashed around.

'That Poppy and Colin are in love and we shouldn't keep them apart.' Ruth smiled up at Tom to let him know that she knew exactly what he was asking. He leaned down and kissed her gently before pulling her into his arms. They stayed as they were for so long that the dogs started barking at them. They broke apart laughing and a little breathless.

'We tell them that you and I have sorted things out between us,' Ruth said, smiling at the idea, since she was sure her friends would be able to work that out for themselves by taking one look at the couple. 'And that we are looking into what has happened but we feel there is more to it.'

Tom nodded before taking Ruth's hand again.

'Thank you.'

'You don't need to thank me.'

'Not just for what you are going to tell the others. For seeing clearly enough to realise that Jeremy is not behind all this. For a moment I thought I was losing my mind, that I would have to sack him or . . .' Tom couldn't bring himself to finish the sentence and Ruth squeezed his hand.

'I am sure he isn't and we will get this whole thing sorted out.' Ruth closed her eyes briefly in an act of hope that she was right.

The walked on together and took the path to the sanctuary. Barbara and Joe were sitting on the bench and Poppy ran towards them before throwing herself into Joe's arms. Joe scooped her up and kissed her.

'Now, you daft lass, what were you doing falling into old holes?' Poppy licked his nose in reply. Joe put her down and Poppy turned to Barbara for some more fussing. Colin trotted up and Joe treated him to a belly rub.

'And you are a very good boy,' he told Colin.

'There's tea in the pot and cake on the side,' Barbara said. 'Glad to see you have worked things out,' she whispered into Ruth's ear before giving her a knowing smile. Ruth didn't even blush. She wasn't embarrassed, just blissfully happy.

'I'll get the tea,' Tom said before disappearing into the cottage.

'Is Poppy all right?' Joe asked, even though Ruth knew he had run his hands all over her to check for himself.

'She seems none the worse for wear, although I think a bath is maybe in order.'

'You're going to have no luck keeping these two apart,' Joe said, fussing both dogs at the same time. 'But looks like that won't be a problem.' Joe was smiling and Ruth smiled back.

'No, I think not,' she said, trying to hold in the happiness that felt like it was going to burst out of her.

'And what about the other stuff?' Joe said, ignoring Barbara's warning look.

'We are investigating. It doesn't quite add up.'

'Doesn't it now?' Joe said drily.

'Do you think Jeremy is particularly tech savvy?' Ruth asked, looking at directly at Joe, who frowned.

'That man couldn't use a sat nav if I wasn't there to do it all for him,' Joe said with a dismissive snort.

'So what are the chances that he would know how to post comments on the village website?'

Ruth knew she was challenging Joe a bit, but also that she needed to. This was step one in getting him and Jeremy to talk over what happened all those years ago.

Joe stared at her and she didn't need him to speak to know that she had put doubt in his mind and that's all she wanted to do.

She wasn't about to tell him that Jeremy had confessed. She wasn't going to tell anyone about that until she had figured out why he would take on the blame for something she was sure he wasn't capable of doing.

'He probably got one of the kids to do it for him,' Joe said and his dismissive tone was back.

Ruth looked up as Tom walked up to

the bench and she knew he had heard every word. Tom wordlessly handed her a mug of tea but it was clear his thoughts were elsewhere.

Ruth was desperate to know what he was thinking but didn't want to bring it up in front of the others.

'Well, we should be getting back to it,' Barbara said and it was clear to Ruth that Tom's expression was not lost on her and she flashed Barbara a grateful smile. Joe was oblivious but followed after Barbara.

'What?' Ruth asked. 'I know something has just clicked.'

'Just what Joe said and what you said. You asked who Jeremy might take the blame for and he would do anything for his grandkids.'

Ruth stared. She could almost believe that they had discovered the truth. But there was still one huge question. Why? Why would Jeremy's grandchildren want to ruin the sanctuary?

'The twins?' Ruth asked with a frown. She could picture Tessa and Jacob dashing around in the woods and it didn't seem to fit. And then a thought struck her, she could hardly bear to say it out loud. It couldn't be the kids, it just couldn't.

'Rob,' Tom said and he said it with such conviction that Ruth blinked in surprise.

'But, Tom, it doesn't explain the dumped rubbish.' Ruth tried to swallow the lump in her throat. All she wanted was for it to be over so that she and Tom could put it behind them and get on with their lives, their lives together.

'It's not like the children can drive, and besides, it was a much older lad that collected the rubbish.'

Tom looked at her and she could see the disappointment in his eyes. She knew that he felt the same as she did. But there was fear, too. Fear that they might never find out? Fear that it might never end?

'I was so sure, just for a few moments,' Tom said, sitting heavily on the bench. He shook his head and stared at the ground.

'Well, let's think about this clearly,'

Ruth suggested but Tom continued to study his feet. 'Jeremy said that Rob was always on his computer?'

Tom shrugged which Ruth took to be agreement.

'So we are sure he has the skills to post on to the website?'

'That's the problem. He has the skills and he would do what Jeremy asked, without question. It all stills points to Jeremy.' Tom's voice cracked a little and Ruth reached out for his hand and gave it a squeeze.

'Jeremy seemed genuinely convinced that I had dumped the rubbish.'

'Just covering his tracks,' Tom said morosely.

'Or he did think it was us.'

Tom frowned.

'In that case we still need to figure out who Jeremy is covering for.'

'Maybe,' Ruth said, half lost in thought. Rob really was the prime suspect in terms of who Jeremy might risk everything for but she just couldn't put the pieces together.

'You can't still think it's the kids?'

Now it was Ruth who shrugged.

'The question you need to ask yourself is whether Jeremy would risk his future and the future of his family for anyone else? He must have known there was a chance that you would fire him,' Ruth pointed out.

Tom leaned back in on the bench so that his back was resting on the wall behind him.

'OK, I agree with that but why would Rob want to do it? What could he possibly have against you and the wildlife sanctuary? You've never even met him.'

'That's what we need to find out,' Ruth said and Tom looked at her. After a few heartbeats he nodded.

'And how do we do that?'

'We go back to Jeremy's and ask him.'

'If you're right and it is Rob, then Jeremy is never going to let that happen.'

Ruth knew that Tom was right.

'You said that Jeremy always goes home to see the kids after school?'

Tom nodded.

'But presumably he starts work before they leave for school?'

Tom nodded again.

'Then I think we need to pay Rob a visit tomorrow morning, before school.'

'We'll have to be careful. It is possible that Rob has nothing to do with it.'

'True, but I suspect if I come with you, we might be able to tell. It's one thing to target a person anonymously, it's another if you come face to face with them.'

'Tomorrow morning then,' Tom said, getting to his feet. He pulled Ruth to hers and kissed her. Once again Ruth felt like the moon had covered the sun and then he stepped away with a smile on his face, despite everything.

'Tomorrow morning,' Ruth said as Tom whistled for Colin and headed back along the path to his land.

Key to the Mystery

Ruth walked to the farmhouse, arriving at seven o'clock to find that Tom was ready with coffee and toast. Poppy and Colin went through their enthusiastic greeting ritual whilst Tom and Ruth had a quick breakfast.

Ruth glanced at her watch and knew they needed to go if they were going to catch Rob with enough time before he needed to leave for school.

She got to her feet and together she and Tom walked to the cottage. They didn't speak, since neither of them knew what to say. If it wasn't Rob, Jeremy would be furious if he discovered that they had confronted him, especially when they had chosen a time when they knew Jeremy wouldn't be there.

But they had no choice, not really. Everyone would be stuck in that moment of Jeremy's confession if they didn't get to the bottom of things.

When they arrived at the cottage the

front door was standing open. Jacob, already dressed in his school uniform, was sitting on the tyre swing pushing himself back and forth.

'Morning, Jake!' Tom shouted and was rewarded with a wave and a grin but Jacob was clearly determined to fit in as much fun as possible before school and so kept swinging.

A woman's face appeared at the door and Ruth guessed this was Jeremy's daughter.

'Hi,' she said with a smile. 'Dad headed out early this morning.'

'I thought he might have, Gina. We've actually come to have a quick word with Rob.'

Gina nodded slowly, looking confused but she called for Rob and there was a clatter of feet on the wooden stairs.

'I heard you, Mum, I'm coming,' Rob grumbled.

Ruth caught the first sight of him and was instantly reminded of his grandfather. He was tall like Jeremy, but he hadn't filled out yet. He had the same slightly unruly hair and a similar expression to his grandad, as if he was permanently prepared to be disappointed.

'I'm not even late.' Rob looked as if he was going to say more but fell silent when he caught sight of Tom and then Ruth.

'Rob, Gina, this is my friend, Ruth. She runs the wildlife sanctuary.'

'Ruth? Hi,' Gina said, holding out a hand and smiling. 'I've been meaning to bring the twins over to see the place. They are mad about wildlife and have been nagging me since you opened. Unlike Rob here — I'm lucky if I can get him to eat dinner before he disappears upstairs to his computer.'

'Mum,' Rob said, his cheeks colouring, although whether it was from embarrassment or something more, Ruth wasn't sure.

'Tom wants to speak to you,' Gina said and there was the first flicker of suspicion on her face. 'And by the looks of you, I am guessing that you know what it's about.' Gina's expression darkened and Rob seemed to shrink a little under her gaze.

'Come in, both of you. I'll make us some fresh tea and you can tell me all about it.'

With one look from Gina, Rob meekly followed his mum to the kitchen at the back of the house. The back wall was one complete folding door and it stood open to the garden behind.

The kitchen was modern but had character, like an updated farmhouse kitchen. There was a range to one side but it was new, modern version and it had a kettle on one of the hot plates that was whistling away.

Tom and Ruth sat side by side at the long wooden table, which seemed to be a feature in every farmhouse kitchen. Rob took a seat as well but as far away from the pair as possible.

Nobody spoke as Gina made the tea. Gina handed around the tea mugs and took a seat.

'Right then, perhaps one of you would like to tell me what is going on?' Gina glanced at Tom and Ruth but her main focus was her son.

He had now had taken on the colour of a beetroot and was studying the grain of the table as if it were the most interesting thing in the world.

Tom seemed to take pity on Rob, who clearly didn't want to be the first to speak.

'You may be aware that there has been a sort of campaign against the wildlife sanctuary,' Tom said slowly, as if he were picking his words carefully.

'I was and I'm really sorry to hear about that,' Gina said, first looking at Ruth and then flicking her eyes to her son. 'Rob, do you have anything to say about that?' she asked.

'No,' Rob mumbled.

Gina raised an eyebrow and continued to look at her son. Rob wasn't ready to make eye contact but it was obvious that he knew his mum was waiting for him to speak.

'The thing is, Rob,' Tom said and again his words were gentle, 'I spoke to your grandad yesterday and he told me it was him.'

Now Rob did look up, his face red and he looked as if he were making a great effort not to cry.

Gina's face crumpled a little and she sighed.

'Now is the time to tell me exactly what you did, Robert. You and I both know that Grandad would never do that, however much he might have moaned about the place.' Gina flashed Ruth an apologetic smile and Ruth returned it to show that she understood.

'That's just it!' Rob's words came out loudly and in a rush. 'Grandad said the place was going to encourage vermin and make his job harder. He said people didn't understand how the countryside really worked. He was so mad and then he said that she was convincing Tom to believe it all, too.'

'You know Ruth's name, Rob, and we don't call anyone 'she',' Gina reprimanded gently. Rob looked at Ruth and then looked away.

'He even said that *Ruth*,' he said the name as if it was new to him and he wasn't sure how to pronounce it, 'was going to take Tom away from us.' Now Rob was crying for real.

'Even if all of that was true, and you and I both know how your grandad needs to blow off steam, why would you do something like this?

'Posting mean messages, putting up posters. Posters that were blatant lies. I raised you better than that.' It wasn't an accusation but more of a statement and Ruth felt a little in awe of Gina's parenting skills.

'Because I don't want to lose Grandad or Tom,' Rob wailed and then dropped his head on to his arms which he had crossed on the table.

Tom and Ruth exchanged glances. Now it was all starting to make sense. Gina had moved along the bench and pulled Rob into her arms and was whispering quietly so that Ruth couldn't hear what she was saying.

Ruth felt a wave of guilt. She had

wanted to know what was going on and why but all she could see now was a frightened upset little boy and couldn't help feeling she was partly responsible. Tom slipped his hand into hers and gave it a squeeze.

'I'm going to make a phone call and ask a friend to take the twins to school,' Gina said.

'Then Rob and I are going to have a little chat. Perhaps we could meet you at yours at ten and try to sort this out?'

'Of course,' Tom said, 'we'll see you there.'

As Tom walked passed Rob, he gave his shoulder a small squeeze.

'Perhaps you could make sure that my dad is there, too?' Gina asked.

'Will do,' Tom said and he and Ruth walked out of the kitchen.

Neither of them said a word until they were well out of earshot.

'Well, I feel awful,' Ruth said and Tom put her arm around her shoulder and pulled him to her.

'Me, too, but we had to get to the

215

bottom of this — not just for our sake, but for theirs.'

Ruth slipped her arms around Tom and they stood holding each other.

'What are you going to do?' Tom asked softly.

'About what?' Ruth asked confused.

'Well now you know who is behind it.'

'I'm not going to do anything. We're going to talk to Jeremy and Rob and sort this out.'

Ruth could feel Tom let out a breath.

'You didn't actually think I was going to call the police, did you?' Ruth shifted away from Tom so that she could see his face.

'No, but you would be well within your rights to do so.'

'I think the pair of them have been punishing themselves enough, don't you? And besides there's no real harm done, apart from Matilda.'

Tom nodded.

'And she has fully recovered. I know that Rob would never set out to hurt an animal.'

They started to walk together hand in hand.

'But I do have an idea that could serve as a sort of community service,' Ruth said.

'I think they both owe you some hours at the sanctuary,' Tom said with a grin. 'And who knows — maybe we can make a convert out of Jeremy.'

Ruth laughed at the thought of Jeremy becoming a champion of wildlife.

'And to be honest I suspect that Jeremy is desperate to do something to set this straight.'

'There is only one problem with that idea,' Ruth said.

'Joe and Jeremy working together again could be interesting, but perhaps now would be a good time to get them to sort things out between them?' Tom suggested.

'As long as it doesn't turn into a fist fight.'

'How about if I volunteer to referee?' Tom said. 'OK — I hope you've got a whistle.'

Magical Powers

When they got back to the farmhouse, Tom left Ruth to sort out some refreshments as he went out to find Jeremy, who was working somewhere on the farm. Ruth raided the cupboards and found some biscuits and set the kettle on the range.

Gina and Rob were the first to arrive. Rob's eyes were red-rimmed and Ruth couldn't help but feel sorry for him. What he had done was wrong, of course, but she also knew at that age loyalty could get you into some sticky situations.

It was clear to Ruth that Rob loved both Tom and his grandad and that fear had motivated some of his actions. Having lost her own dad, she could relate to that feeling.

'Come in and have a seat. I'm making tea, unless you'd like a cold drink, Rob?'

With an effort Rob looked at her before quickly looking away.

'No, thank you, Ruth. Tea is good,'

Rob said very politely.

'Do you need a hand?' Gina asked and she sounded as nervous as Ruth felt.

'I'm fine, thanks. Tom has gone to find your dad.'

Gina sat beside her son and Ruth busied herself making the tea, hoping that Tom would be back soon. She was sure that she and Gina could be good friends but trying to make small talk in the current situation was not going to be easy.

As if on cue, the door opened and Tom and Jeremy stepped in. Jeremy's face was unreadable but on seeing his grandad, Rob leapt to his feet and threw himself into his arms.

'It's all right, lad. It's all right,' Jeremy said, rubbing Rob's back. 'We'll sort this out, just you wait and see.' Jeremy flicked a glance at Ruth, who smiled reassuringly and gestured for them all to take a seat. Tom sat next to Ruth and everyone looked at each other, waiting for someone else to speak.

'I'll start, then,' Tom said with a small smile. 'So we know that Rob posted the messages and made the posters.' Rob gulped and nodded.

'But we also know why he did it, because he was worried about losing his grandad and maybe that he wouldn't get to see me any more?'

Rob nodded again and sniffed. Gina put an arm around her son's shoulders.

'Well, let's start with that, shall we?' Tom continued. 'Rob, you aren't going to lose me, you'll see as much of me as you can bear and as for your grandad . . .' Tom looked to Jeremy.

'I ain't going nowhere, lad, you know that.'

'But what if you lose your job?' Rob's sniffs turned into a wail and he buried his face in his mum's arms.

'Nobody is losing their job, Rob. Do you really think I could run this place without your grandad?'

Rob looked up and Tom looked straight back at him, reassuring him with his eyes.

'Are you sure, son?' Jeremy asked. 'I wouldn't blame you if you wanted rid of me.'

'We've already talked about this and yes, I'm sure.'

'But even if I've got a criminal record?' Tom looked to Ruth.

'I'm not getting the police involved,' Ruth said firmly. 'There's no need since there won't be any more problems.'

They all looked at Rob who nodded and was starting to look a little less like his world was ending.

'There won't be, and Rob will be grounded without access to his computer for some time,' Gina said, raising an eyebrow at her son daring him to argue but Rob just nodded meekly.

'We'll actually I had an idea about that,' Ruth said and Gina looked up. 'I was thinking that perhaps Rob could come and help out at the sanctuary.'

Gina smiled gratefully.

'I think that would be an excellent way for Rob to make amends.'

Rob nodded and he looked as if that wasn't the worst punishment ever. Perhaps Ruth could convert him to the outdoors after all.

'I'd like to help out, too, if you'll have me. Least I can do,' Jeremy said gruffly.

'I do have one question, though,' Ruth said and everyone looked at her. 'How did you get the rubbish from the tip to here?'

Rob blushed the colour of beetroot and Jeremy fixed him with a hard stare.

'Tell Ruth, lad. Might as well get it all out in the open.'

'I paid a friend from school's brother. He followed you up to the tip and bought the rubbish.' Rob was talking to his knees.

'Where did you get the money?' Gina demanded, looking shocked.

'Dad gave me some,' Rob mumbled.

'I don't think your dad had that in mind when he gave it to you.'

Rob shrugged.

'Wait — are you talking about Jamie?' Gina asked and Rob nodded. 'I've paid him to take rubbish up to the tip because I didn't have the time.'

Rob nodded again and Tom and Ruth

exchanged glances. The last piece of the puzzle had fallen into place.

'Wherever did you come up with the idea to dump rubbish?' Ruth asked.

'Rob overheard me talking about how I thought you might get fed up with all the tip runs and dump it somewhere,' Jeremy said but unlike Rob, he was looking Ruth in the eye.

'I was just letting off steam, talking nonsense but Rob overheard me which is why I take full responsibility for all this. I should watch my mouth.'

'Yes, you should,' Gina said, sounding like Jeremy's parent and not the other way round. This made everyone smile.

'And I shouldn't make such judgements, either. I didn't know what Rob had been up to when I found the rubbish and I was right angry that anyone could do such a thing and in my mind you seemed the most likely offender,' Jeremy said.

'Thank you,' Ruth said. 'I hope by now you know that I am as passionate about preserving the countryside as you are, even if we do approach it differently.'

'I know that now and I'm mighty sorry for not taking the time to find that out.'

Jeremy held out his hand and Ruth shook it solemnly before they both smiled.

'Well, would I be right in assuming that we all want to put this nonsense behind us?' Tom said and he looking as if a weight had been lifted from his shoulders.

Everyone, especially Rob, nodded vigorously.

'When do you want your workers to start?' Gina asked and it was clear she was not going to let that aspect of punishment go.

'How about this evening? After dinner? The evenings are pretty busy for us since most of our guests are nocturnal,' Ruth said with a smile.

'We'll be there,' Jeremy said. 'Now, I best be getting back to work.'

'We probably all should,' Tom agreed. 'I'll come over with the boys tonight if that's OK,' Tom added softly to Ruth.

'Lovely,' Ruth said, feeling like all was right with the world.

That was until she thought about how she was going to persuade Joe and Jeremy to make peace. She sighed to herself as she walked the path home with Poppy at her side. If only those two could find a way to make amends.

If Jeremy would explain and apologise, which Ruth thought he would now, since he seemed to be on a bit of a run. But the real problem might be whether Joe could forgive and put so many years of bitterness and hurt behind him. If he couldn't then life would remain difficult.

Jeremy was coming to help out at the sanctuary and the last thing Ruth wanted was for Joe to feel that he could no longer be a part of it.

'We are just going to have to figure out a way to make this all happen,' Ruth told Poppy.

'If we don't, things will always be a little bit difficult. And if Tom and I want a future together we need our two father figures to at least tolerate each other.'

Poppy barked and Ruth thought Poppy agreed. After all, she suspected Poppy felt about Colin the way she felt about Tom. Well, at least that was one less problem. The dogs behaved like star-crossed lovers so would have no problem at all with her and Tom spending more time together.

'We'll figure it out, Pops. We have to,' Ruth said, trying to sound confident and desperately racking her brains for a plan.

When Ruth got back to the sanctuary there was lots to do. A couple of abandoned fox cubs had come in and both needed some veterinary attention. Joe wasn't on the day shift as he was off visiting his sister but would be back for the evening shift.

The evening shift was not something that Ruth particularly wanted to think about. As hard as she had tried, no plan had come to mind. She just couldn't predict how Joe would react and if she was being honest she didn't really blame him.

Jeremy had forced Joe from a job he

loved based on incorrect information, it was true but would Joe be able to hear and accept that? Ruth wasn't sure.

She felt a bit like Juliet in the tragic romance, hoping to reunite two warring families. She shook her head to shift the idea — everyone knew how that turned out. Perhaps she should speak to Joe before Jeremy arrived. Give him a sort of pep talk to try and make him understand.

'Ruth? We've had a phone call from the main site and they have decided that we can take the donkey and pony. I've told them the paddock is ready and they should bring them over, if that's OK?' Joe asked.

Ruth was glad that he had called from the office so he couldn't see her jump at the sound of his voice.

'OK, but I'll need to make a run for feed,' Ruth replied, trying to focus on work and not the evening events.

'They're going to bring enough for a couple of days. I'll pick some up on my way in tomorrow,' Joe said.

'Good. Any problems we should know about?' Ruth said, crossing the yard to the office so they no longer had to shout.

'Still need some feeding up but they're in a much better state than they were.'

'I think we can manage that.' Ruth grinned at Joe, knowing that the man had a bit of a soft spot for donkeys.

Maybe the new arrivals would soften the news that his arch enemy was coming over to help out at the sanctuary. Ruth felt her grin slip a little. Donkeys were amazing but she wasn't sure they could do that.

She still hadn't been able to come up with any kind of plan to make the two men talk to each other, or listen to each other, which she suspected was the bit that was needed the most. With a sigh she turned back to the list of urgent jobs that needed doing. Perhaps if she forgot about it, her brain would conjure up some sort of magic plan.

★ ★ ★

228

The truck pulling the trailer arrived late afternoon and some of the volunteers had stayed beyond their allotted time to meet the new arrivals.

Ruth greeted Ken, who was another volunteer that worked at the main centre, as he stepped out of the cab.

'The place looks amazing, Ruth!' he said as he scanned the yard and the many sheds that had been built to house the animals.

'Thanks. We've all worked really hard.'

'Ken,' Joe said as he appeared and shook hands with the extremely tall man with military cropped hair, 'you wait till you see the paddock. It'll be perfect for our new guests.'

Ken and Joe walked around and pulled down the ramp before each taking a bridle and walking the pony and the donkey out into the yard. Ruth cast an expert eye over them. Joe had been right. They needed feeding up but otherwise they seemed in reasonable condition.

'Any interest?' Joe asked and Ruth smiled. Joe had a small bungalow with no land to speak of so he couldn't take the two new arrivals but that didn't mean he wouldn't be happy for the two to retire permanently to the sanctuary.

'Nah, mate. Nobody seems to want them both and we don't want to split them up.'

Joe and Ken walked the two animals to the paddock before opening the gate and letting them go. The volunteers all lined up around the fence watching the pair kicking up their heels in the wide open space. Ruth knew the pair would be spoilt rotten by everyone and it was no less than they deserved.

Ruth turned at the sound of another vehicle pulling up beside the horse trailer. She knew who it was, even before she could make out the truck. Tom climbed out from the driver's seat and waved. Ruth felt her heart drum in her chest at the sight of him. By the look on his face, he was as pleased to see her as she was to see him.

Rob climbed out the back and went to stand by his grandad. Ruth struggled with separate emotions. She was glad to see them both, glad to be able to introduce them to the work they were trying to achieve here but equally dreading how Joe might react when he saw Jeremy.

Ruth walked over to say hello as Ken climbed back in his truck and manoeuvred his way out of the yard.

'New guests?' Tom asked, hugging Ruth.

'Yes, the main centre had a donkey and pony that needed pasture. Do you want to come and meet them?'

Ruth's question was directed at Rob but she couldn't help but notice that Jeremy's eyes lit up. They walked together towards the paddock. The group of volunteers who had stayed to watch had started to disperse. Joe was standing on the bottom rung of the fence and giving the donkey a good scratch between the ears.

'What's his name?' Rob said, climbing up besides Joe.

'He doesn't have one yet, lad, but maybe we can come up with one between us?' Joe said, smiling at the boy. He looked over his shoulder to Ruth and that was when his expression twisted into one of intense dislike.

'What's he doing 'ere?' Joe demanded.

Ruth opened her mouth to speak but was beaten to it.

'I've come to help out. It's the least that Rob and I can do after all that's happened,' Jeremy said. His voice wasn't exactly warm but it had at least lost some of the accusatory tone.

Joe looked from Jeremy to Ruth to Rob and even though Ruth doubted he had the full picture he seemed to have put together enough of the pieces to understand some of what had happened. He nodded and then shrugged as if it didn't matter to him whether Jeremy was there or not.

'But before I get to work, you and I need to have a talk,' Jeremy said.

Ruth held her breath and she could feel Tom stiffen beside her. Could it really be that simple?

'And why would I want to listen to

anything you've got to say?' Joe said, keeping his voice low. Ruth suspected he didn't want to get into a shouting match with Rob there.

'Because I want to make things right, you old fool. The least you can do is hear me out.'

The two men glared at each other but nobody said anything.

'Rob, why don't you come and see the young birds? It's feeding time and you might want to have a go.'

Rob looked uncertainly at his grandad who nodded that he should go and so reluctantly Rob followed Ruth and Tom. Once Rob was set up with his tweezers and plate of meal worms, Ruth and Tom stepped outside.

'Do you think we should go back and make sure no punches are thrown?' Ruth asked.

'I think they need to sort this one out themselves,' Tom said but he kept glancing towards the paddock himself so Ruth knew he was as concerned as she was.

'Do you really think after all these

years that they could actually be friends?'

Tom pulled Ruth into his arms and kissed her gently.

'Friends might be a stretch but we could hope for a grudging tolerance for each other.'

Ruth giggled. It seemed impossible but it really was the last piece of the picture that could be a perfect life together. Less than a month before it felt like her new life was in danger of falling apart but now, if their two father figures could just work things out maybe she and Tom could have their happy ever after.

'Whatever happens,' Tom said sounding serious now, 'I love you and that won't change even if those two don't get on. I won't let it stand between us.'

'Me neither,' Ruth said although she couldn't help but wish that Joe and Jeremy would find a way to tolerate each other. They were such an important part of her life, and Tom's.

'Do you think we should go and check?' Ruth whispered.

'Well, I don't hear any shouting so

maybe that's a good sign?'

Tom threw his arm around Ruth's shoulder and she slipped an arm around his waist. It felt like they were two halves who had finally found their missing piece. They walked down towards the paddock.

Poppy and Colin were sitting side by side, watching the pony gallop around its new pasture. Tom and Ruth stopped in their tracks.

'Well, would you look at that?' Tom said quietly.

Ruth couldn't quite believe what she was seeing — Joe and Jeremy standing closer together than they had in years. Jeremy was fussing the donkey's ears and Joe was running a hand down the donkey's back.

'I was wrong, donkeys do have magical powers,' Ruth said softly. Tom looked at her quizzically and then they both laughed. It was only now that the two older men looked up.

'We've come up with a name,' Joe said.

Ruth tried not to let her mouth drop

open. Had Joe just said 'we'?

'Oh, yes?' Tom said.

'Bobby,' Joe said.

'After the great Bobby Moore,' Jeremy added. 'No good standing their gawking, Ruthie. We've got work to do. Jeremy's going to help me get the feed down to the troughs. You and Tom see to the hoglets.'

Ruth nodded and could do nothing but stare as Jeremy and Joe walked off.

'What just happened?' she finally managed to say. 'If I'd have known all it would take was a donkey, I would have found one months ago.'

A Very Special Day

Ruth stepped out of her cottage, feeling nervous but excited. Barbara and Sam followed her out, making sure that her dress was straight and making finishing touches to the fresh sweet peas which adorned Ruth's hair.

'Oh, lass, you look beautiful,' Joe said, holding out his arm to her.

Ruth's pale cream dress was simple, with a layer of delicate flowered lace. It was her mum's dress and so there had been no question of her wearing anything else.

'You're making both your folks so proud today,' Joe said a little gruffly and she knew that he was fighting some warring emotions, just as she was. Ruth nodded as she fought back a few tears.

'They are both here with you,' Barbara said, handing Ruth her bouquet of hand-tied flowers.

Ruth felt for her locket, one that Tom had bought for her and found a photo of her mum and dad to put inside. Ruth had been speechless and moved all at the same time and she knew that both her parents would thoroughly have approved of Tom.

'If you're ready, lass?'

Poppy appeared beside her, wearing a silky bandana, the same soft violet as Barbara and Sam, her maids of honour, were wearing.

'Anyone would think she was the one getting wed,' Joe said with a chuckle as Poppy paced up and down.

'I think she thinks she is,' Ruth said, giving Poppy a quick scratch behind the ears.

'The guests are waiting,' Sam said and she raised a hand in the air.

On cue the traditional wedding march sounded. All eyes travelled to the paddock which had chairs laid out in rows facing a rose covered arch where the local vicar was waiting. Bobby and Daisy, as Rob had named the pony, were being held by a beaming Rob.

Ruth walked holding Joe's arm and

then she caught sight of Tom and it took her breath away. He was wearing a navy suit with a violet tie. He looked nervous and excited, and very handsome. Colin was sitting beside him, with his violet bandana.

Ruth and Joe reached the aisle that had been marked out and Poppy trotted ahead to be greeted by a very enthusiastic Colin. All the guests laughed and so Ruth walked down the aisle to the sweet sound of giggles. At the end of the aisle, Joe leaned in and kissed Ruth before passing her hand to Tom's outstretched one.

'You look stunning,' Tom whispered.

'You don't look bad yourself,' Ruth said.

The ceremony started and Ruth felt like time had stopped. Before she knew it they were married.

'You may now kiss the bride,' the vicar said with a warm smile.

Tom leaned in and Ruth felt like she melted in his arms. Jeremy and Joe shook hands, clapping each other on back as if they had been friends for decades and Poppy and Colin skipped up the aisle.

The guests all stood and cheered and Tom and Ruth watched as they all made their way across the fields to the farmhouse where the reception was to be held. Ruth leaned up against Tom who had his arms wrapped around her.

'Penny for your thoughts, Mrs McMillan?'

Ruth smiled at the sound of her new name.

'Just wondering how we got so lucky that everything worked out.'

'It's a miracle,' he whispered softly. 'And you know what comes next?' Ruth turned to face him. 'We are all going to live happily ever after.' Ruth looked into Tom's eyes before standing on her tiptoes and kissing him. Colin and Poppy barked in agreement and Ruth and Tom broke apart to smile.

'All of us,' Ruth said before they started walking across the fields with their dogs running beside them.